CRAB TOWN

Also by **Carlton Mellick III**

Satan Burger
Electric Jesus Corpse
Sunset With a Beard (stories)
Razor Wire Pubic Hair
Teeth and Tongue Landscape
The Steel Breakfast Era
The Baby Jesus Butt Plug
Fishy-fleshed
The Menstruating Mall
Ocean of Lard (with Kevin L. Donihe)
Punk Land
Sex and Death in Television Town
Sea of the Patchwork Cats
The Haunted Vagina
Cancer-cute (Avant Punk Army Exclusive)
War Slut
Sausagey Santa
Ugly Heaven, Beautiful Hell (with Jeffrey Thomas)
Adolf in Wonderland
Ultra Fuckers
Cybernetrix
The Egg Man
Apeshit
The Faggiest Vampire
The Cannibals of Candyland
Warrior Wolf Women of the Wasteland
The Kobold Wizard's Dildo of Enlightenment +2
Zombies and Shit

CRAB TOWN

Carlton Mellick III

Eraserhead Press
Portland, OR

ERASERHEAD PRESS
205 NE BRYANT
PORTLAND, OR 97211

WWW.ERASERHEADPRESS.COM

ISBN: 1-936383-41-1

Printed in the USA.

AUTHOR'S NOTE

Books written by a lot of people I know are usually produced in this order:

1) the book is written
2) the book is titled
3) the back cover description is written
4) cover art is obtained

When I wrote *Crab Town*, I did all of this in reverse. My usual cover artist Ed Mironiuk had done this image of the girl on the bomb that I really liked. I decided I wanted to write a book based on the image. He was cool with the idea and even gave some plot suggestions, some of which I went with. Then I came up with a description for the book that went with the art. Then I called it Crab Town, because I thought the title somehow went perfectly with the art for no explainable reason. Then, finally, I actually wrote the book.

Crab Town is the first novella I've written since *Ultra Fuckers*, which came out about 9 books ago. I needed to get back into writing them because in my opinion 100 page novellas are the perfect length for bizarro fiction stories. After writing the two epics *Warrior Wolf Women of the Wasteland* and *Zombies and Shit*, I thought it was about time to write some shorter books for a change before moving on to the next epic I plan to write, *Seven Cyborgs*.

I went into this book wanting to just write a fun, dumb little bizarro bank heist story. But I think it became a little more than that. If there were a message to Crab Town it would be: debt is the scariest fucking thing in the world. Well, maybe it's not scarier than say a tidal wave made of sharks and chainsaws heading toward your children, but it's one of the most realistic things to fear because it's the most likely thing that can, and will, fuck over your whole life.

Debt is the reason there aren't too many full time writers

or artists anymore. As a full time writer living my dream, I can have it all taken away from me at any moment. It's happened to tons of writers that I've known. It's called: not having health insurance. If you're a full time writer you're not getting health insurance. You're lucky enough to be able to pay rent with the small amount of money you're making. All it takes is to have a medical emergency, which is bound to happen someday, and without health insurance those hospital bills are going to hit you with debt so hard you'll have to get two back-to-back day jobs in order to pay them off.

Fuck that shit!

Real life just isn't set up for certain kinds of people, and artists/writers are one of them. Living your dream is worth the risk, sure, but you'll often find yourself getting the shit end of the stick. So here is a story about several types of people getting the shit end of the stick. But these guys are far from living their dream. In the world of Crab Town, dreams were nuked a long time ago.

- Carlton Mellick III 01/21/2011 4:58pm

JOHNNY
BALLOON

Most people are poor these days, but Johnny is so poor he can't even afford to pay for gravity. They call him Johnny Balloon. That's basically what he is. A balloon. There are a lot of balloon people these days. The worse the economy gets, the more balloon people you are likely to see walking (or floating) around town.

Only the most desperate individuals shed their humanity to become balloon people. The procedure is free. They basically scoop out all of your insides and turn your mind into a sentient gas which is then put into a human-shaped balloon body.

On the upside, a balloon person will never need to eat or sleep ever again. They never age. They essentially become immortal. But balloon people don't have the operation because they want to achieve immortality (nobody would choose to live immortally as a balloon); they do it so they can sell their organs, which usually can be sold at a pretty high price. Healthy (or even slightly healthy) organs are always in high demand these days, especially due to all the radiation damage that people have suffered ever since the most recent nuclear war.

Johnny Balloon waves at the people he passes, as he walks down the sidewalk in the middle class district of Freedom City. The people do not wave back, but instead inch away from him with quivering eyes. All balloon people are considered creepy, but Johnny is an especially creepy balloon person. It is because his face is in a permanent smile, so wide that it makes him look like some kind of demented clown doll. When the doctor took the picture that was to be graphed onto Johnny's balloon head, he suggested that

Johnny make a normal face, without expressing any emotion. But Johnny didn't like that idea. He'd rather look eternally cheerful than express nothing but apathy for the rest of his life.

Johnny tried to make the happiest, most cheerful face possible when the picture was taken. But, after he was converted into a balloon, Johnny realized he might have smiled a little too wide. While looking in the mirror, squeaking his rubber hand against his face, he noticed his smile did make him look a tad bit on the insane side. He still hoped people would realize, after they got to know him, that he was a happy balloon man and not really an insane balloon man.

Most balloon people do not have happy faces painted on their balloons because they usually don't have anything to be happy about. Nobody enjoys being a balloon. Even the most optimistic balloon people eventually succumb to depression.

This unending depression in balloon people usually comes the first month they get their gravity bill. The doctors never tell their patients that they'll have to pay for gravity before they get the operation. The balloon people go through with the procedure because they believe they'll never have to worry about money ever again. But in order to get the gravity device connected to their feet, balloon people must pay a fee of $1750 a month or risk floating away.

All the money the balloon person makes selling his organs usually goes straight to paying off his gravity bills. After a year or so, the balloon person will run out of cash and have his gravity shut off. That is, unless the person has a job, which is unlikely because so few companies hire balloons. The balloon person would have been far better off if he never went through with the operation.

But Johnny tries to be optimistic. He tries to be happy. Even though he was screwed over by yet another scheme of the medical industry, he tries to think it was all for the best. That's the kind of guy Johnny Balloon is. He doesn't cry (not that he can cry) over the fact that he can no longer afford to pay for gravity. He figures a way around it.

Instead of spending his last $2000 on one more month of gravity, he said, "Screw gravity!" Then he got rid of his gravity device and saved the rest of his money for entertainment.

"Who needs it, anyway?" he said, as he tied his balloon string to a cinder block in order to weigh himself down. Now he carries the block around with him wherever he goes.

Johnny Balloon is on his way to the bank, but he's thinking of seeing a movie today. Johnny loves going to the movies. It's one of the few things a balloon can enjoy. Unfortunately, balloon people are usually not very welcome in movie theaters. The other movie-goers think their squeaky balloon sounds are annoying and ruin the movie-going experience. For this reason, Johnny tries to see movies during the day, when the theater is mostly empty.

Holding a newspaper over his cinder block as he walks, he checks to see what is playing at the town theater. He opens his knapsack and pulls out a watch. It's still early. He has plenty of time, if things go smoothly. He puts the watch back into the bag, careful not to cut himself on anything sharp within.

Since balloon people have their clothes permanently painted onto their bodies, they don't have any pockets. They have to store everything in bags they carry. It is possible for balloons to wear watches, but Johnny would rather not. He thinks it feels weird on his wrist.

Johnny stops in his tracks. He looks at the ground. While reading the newspaper, he wasn't watching where he was going. He almost steps on broken glass. Just like a regular balloon, Johnny Balloon can easily be popped. One little prick will cause his balloon body to explode.

Scanning the ground, there are several broken beer bottles all around him. Slivers of glass cover the sidewalk and the street on both sides. Johnny folds up the newspaper and puts it in his bag, then carefully backs away. He'd rather play it safe and take the long way to the bank than try to tiptoe through the shards of glass.

But as he walks backward, he hears a *clink* as he kicks some glass with the back of his heel. When he turns around, he realizes there are more broken bottles behind him as well. He wonders how he got through all of that without popping. He must have accidentally stepped in all the right places without paying any attention.

"It must be my lucky day," he says.

But then he realizes he's trapped within the circle of glass. He squeak-rubs his forehead, contemplating his best course of action. One of the problems with getting rid of the gravity devices that were attached to his feet is that they used to act as protective footwear. Before, he could have walked over this glass with no worry. Now, it's not so easy to walk safely through the streets.

Examining carefully, he realizes he's going to have to jump over it. Safety is only five feet away. He believes he can make it, even if he won't get much of a running start.

He bends his knees, flexing his rubber legs with a *squeak-squeak*.

"Come on, Johnny Balloon," he tells himself. "You can do it."

Then he jumps, but with the weight of the cinder block in his arms he doesn't go very far.

"You *can't* do it," he cries, in midair.

As he watches his feet drop toward a sharp blade of glass, Johnny drops the cinder block. With the loss of weight, his body flies away from the ground, spinning toward the sky. Once he's three stories up, his balloon string goes taut and ceases his ascent. He rolls over in the air and looks down at the people walking by on the street below. None of them seem to notice that he's floating above them. None of them offer to help him out.

"No problem," he says. "I've prepared for this…"

He swims through the air and grabs the string below him. This is something he's practiced in his apartment several times before.

"All I have to do is climb down…"

One hand after another, he pulls himself down the string.

"Easy peasy…"

But once he's seven feet from the ground, he isn't quite sure what to do from there. The ground is still covered in glass. He tries calling out to the people walking by, but they just ignore him, going around, annoyed that he's taking up their sidewalk.

"Fine, I don't need help. I'm sure I can figure this out on my own…"

He tries tugging on his balloon string to pull it across the sidewalk, out of the glass. It moves an inch.

"There you go, Johnny Balloon," he says. "It's going to work just fine…"

He pulls it again, harder, moving it a whole foot across the ground this time.

"You're the smartest balloon in town," he says with a giggle.

He tugs on it again. The string breaks.

"Wuh…" Johnny says, as he sees the end of the string separate from the cinder block.

He floats further into the air, screaming for help, trying to swim-fly, trying to grab onto the light post that is only another arm's reach away. Nobody even looks at him. His gaseous brain spins inside his hollow shell of a head as he drifts higher and higher toward the blue abyss above.

When he was a kid in grade school, Johnny learned about the Great Depression in history class.

He asked his teacher, "What's the difference between

13

the Great Depression and our times?"

The teacher looked out the window at the war torn city and said, "Our times are a heck of a lot worse."

Johnny didn't really understand the definition of the word *depression*, even after his school had closed down due to lack of funding. He regularly heard people call the current era the *Greater* Depression, but his father said a more apt term for it would be the *Infinite* Depression…

"Because there's no hope of ever getting out of this one…"

When Johnny became an adult, the depression only got worse. He lost his job at the canning factory and had to move to the Crab Town area of Freedom City, where all the other jobless people live. The Great Depression Era had Hoovervilles. These days, there are Crab Towns.

"Why's it called a Crab Town, anyway?" Johnny asked one of his neighbors.

The neighbor was an elderly woman suffering from radiation sickness. She coughed a pool of blood into her palm and wiped it on a crusty brown t-shirt before answering, "Because everyone in this section of city lives in CRABs."

CRAB stands for Citizen Renovated Abandoned Building. After the end of the war, once neither side could afford to pay for any more bombs to drop, the government proposed the idea of Crab Towns.

"If you can renovate it, you can own it." That was what they said at the time.

Since many people were out of work and living in the streets, and most of the bombed sections of the city had been abandoned, it seemed like a good way to rebuild the cities while at the same time give the less fortunate citizens somewhere to live. Unfortunately, those who were in need of homes did not have the resources to repair buildings that had been partially leveled by atomic blasts.

But Johnny was happy in his apartment in Crab Town. He used a tarp instead of a south wall, there wasn't any running water, and he could see into the apartments below and above him via multiple holes, but it was home. And Johnny kind of liked it. That is, until he was so desperate for money that he decided to have the operation to become a balloon man. His apartment wasn't a very happy place after that. Even those living in Crabs didn't like having balloon people around.

Johnny grabs hold of a windowsill six stories up. His legs dangling up in the air above his head as he looks inside. There's a young naked woman near the window, washing soap from her face and semi-pregnant belly with a hose attached to her kitchen sink.

When he sees her, Johnny yells, "*Help!*" as he tries to climb inside.

The woman sees him and shrieks. She grabs a mildew-encrusted towel and covers her breasts. The cloth is too small to hide the rest of her body, which is coated in razor scars.

"Please," Johnny cries, his fingers slipping. "Please…"

The woman sneers at him. "Get out of here you perverted creep!"

"No, that's not it…" Johnny says.

Then she lifts her large sawdust-covered foot and kicks him in the face. His balloon head bounces off of her heel, launching him out of the window.

"I'm floating away!" Johnny yells.

"Serves you right!" The woman pulls a knife out of the kitchen sink and tosses it through the window at him.

The blade barely misses Johnny's shoulder.

"Don't do that!" he says.

She throws another knife at him, then a few forks. Johnny's lucky she's a bad aim. He drifts up past her window before she can pop him.

A breeze comes in and blows him down the street, toward a crowd of people crossing a busy intersection.

"Help me!" Johnny cries, but nobody bothers looking up.

He blows past them and goes over another group of people down the block.

"Help!"

A fat guy with bloody teeth looks up from his hot dog to watch Johnny's plight for entertainment. The man smiles and then takes another bite of hot dog.

The balloon string gets tangled up in a tree and catches Johnny from moving any further. His body just whips around in the breeze. After ten minutes of begging for help from passersby, he gives up. He realizes he can't rely on anyone but himself in this city. He grabs his string and pulls himself in toward the nearest tree branch.

When he gets to the bottom of the trunk, he fills his knapsack with pieces of rubble from the street. Lucky for him, the streets are always filled with debris. Even the buildings in the middle class side of town are falling apart. Once his bag is the right weight to keep him on the ground, he unties his string from the branch.

"Thank God that wasn't a pine tree…"

He waits for a large black sewer crab to cross the sidewalk before continuing on. The sewer crab looks a little too snippy. After all that he's already been through, Johnny decides he's going to have to play it safe for the rest of the day.

When Johnny Balloon enters the bank, the place is crowded, even for Liberty Bank. He scans the people in lines, a mixture of middle class and working class people, with a handful of Crab Town residents sprinkled in. It's going to be hard for him to get out of here in time to catch a movie.

There are two burly guards staring Johnny down as he gets into a line. Cops and security especially hate balloon people. There's no reason why. They just can't stand the floating creeps. A man in a yellow hat leans against a wall in the back of the room. He also stares Johnny down. The guy has to be an undercover guard. Every bank has one now. There are too many robberies these days, too many desperate people, and bank security isn't what it used to be.

The corporate banks went out of business a long time ago. Now, only a few private banks exist in Freedom City. These banks are always packed and always getting hit by desperate criminals.

After ten minutes of waiting, Johnny realizes something is holding up the line. It has hardly moved. A middle-aged woman is at the front of the line, holding everything up. She is a pink lady: pink dress, pink shoes, and pink bow in her hair. Wealthy women like to wear pink or other bright colors. It is a symbol of high class. Nobody else in the room has clothes as bright and clean and new as hers. Most of them don't even own washing machines.

She is the bank manager's wife.

That's when Johnny realizes the woman isn't even in line. She's just chatting up the teller. And the teller, an older woman with orange curly hair and white glasses, ignores her customers to gossip with her boss's wife.

"What the fuck…" Johnny says, but the women are too far up there to hear him.

The pink woman has a son with her. By the looks of it, the kid is a real brat. He runs around the room with a toy metal airplane, making airplane noises at the top of his lungs. He charges at the people in line and makes machine gun noises at them, as if his little plane is gunning them down. The mother ignores her kid, too wrapped up in conversation to care that he's being a nuisance to everyone around them.

The kid runs across the line shooting everyone. When he passes by Johnny, the balloon man inches away. Kids always make Johnny nervous. They are too unpredictable. You never know what they're going to do, especially the ones who have parents that let them run wild in public.

There are three other balloon people in line with Johnny. They look like newbies to balloon life, probably at the bank to take out money to pay their gravity bill. The balloon woman standing near the front of the line doesn't see it coming when the bratty kid swoops in behind her and slams the tip of his toy plane into her back.

The balloon woman pops. Her hollow body explodes into shreds of rubber that sprinkle in the air like confetti. Johnny gasps, but he's the only one. The kid looks at what he's done with a wide open mouth, and then he bursts into giddy laughter.

Nobody in the room seems to care. In fact, a lot of the people seem happy that the line is finally moving a bit. The mother continues chatting with her friend, as if nothing's happened. She has to be aware that her kid has just murdered a balloon woman, but it doesn't seem to be that urgent of an issue.

If you act fast you can save a balloon person after she pops. You can suck her gaseous form into a vacuum and return her to a balloon body, but nobody does anything. Not the security guards, not even the other balloon people. The woman's gaseous form rises to the ceiling and then is sucked through the air vents, to be sprayed outside and dissipated into the atmosphere.

The kid realizes that he's just found a new game to play. He creeps over to the next balloon person in line. It is an old man balloon. He glances down at the boy with his blank frozen expression.

"BOOOM!" the kid cries, as he pops the old man.

The kid is in tears with laughter as the line moves up another person.

"Kyle!" the mother says to him. "Keep it down!"

But that's all she does. She turns back to her friend, ignoring her kid again. The boy has no intention of listening to his mother, as he creeps down the line looking for another balloon to pop.

Johnny crouches down behind the person ahead of him, hiding himself from the boy. A black woman behind Johnny cringes when his butt rubs against her purse. She gives him a look like she's about to pop him herself, just for getting too close. Her eyes widen with anger and she shakes her head, grumbling some obscenities under her breath.

The other balloon man also crouches down to hide from the kid, but he's a very large balloon with a big round belly. The boy spots him right away, sneaks up to him with his airplane pointed at his stomach.

"No, don't!" the balloon man cries, backing away.

The kid yells "BOOOM!" and charges him. The man runs backwards, screaming for help, but everyone just laughs at the fat balloon trying to get away from the kid. A couple of women smile and sigh, as if what the kid is doing is so cute and precious. The balloon man runs toward the door, but one of the security officers trips him.

The guard laughs at the balloon man as the boy jumps on top of him plane-first. The fat guy screams one last time as he pops, and the kid falls through his confetti-flesh onto the ground.

As the boy rolls around on the floor, laughing, his mother charges him.

"That's enough, young man!" she says, grabbing him by the arm.

The second the woman touches the boy, he shrieks at the top of his lungs as if her hand is made of acid. She drags him through the line, right past Johnny. As the kid goes by, he tries to swing his airplane at him, but Johnny is just a bit out of reach.

"No! No!" the kid yells as his mom pulls him away. "I want to pop the other one! I want to pop the other one!"

The woman sits him down in a chair.

"Do you like embarrassing me like this?" the woman yells at the child. "Do you think it's fun to make me look like an idiot?"

The boy ignores her. "Just one more! Just let me pop one more!"

"No," she says. "Now stay in this seat while I go see Daddy. If you're not here when I get back you're not getting a new toy after lunch."

The kid cries out, gargling words that don't make any sense. As she walks away, he pouts and kicks his legs, striking at the air with vengeance. Johnny wipes his forehead with relief.

After the mother disappears into one of the back offices, the boy becomes silent. Johnny Balloon advances in the line, but he can feel the boy's eyes watching him every step he takes. He can tell the boy is trying to figure out a way to pop him without getting caught. Johnny decides not to take his eyes off of the kid. If he gets out of that chair Johnny plans to run.

When Johnny gets to the front of the line, the teller with the orange curly hair rolls her eyes.

She says, "Great, now I've got to deal with a fucking balloon."

To most balloon people, being called a *balloon* is considered offensive. But Johnny doesn't mind it. He thinks the term is rather appropriate.

Johnny unzips his knapsack and pulls out his wallet. "I'd like to make a withdrawal. Fifty dollars."

He hands her his bank account number. Nothing is run by computers anymore, so she looks up his account folder via filing cabinet.

"I'm sorry, sir," she says, "but your account balance is at negative nineteen-hundred-and-twenty-three dollars."

"What?" Johnny shakes his head. "That's impossible. I should have at least fifteen hundred dollars left. Look at the records."

The teller intentionally uses her middle finger to push her white glasses up her nose. Then she goes to her records. As she pages through his account history, sighing loudly to express her annoyance, Johnny turns to keep his eye on the boy.

The kid is no longer in his chair. He is sneaking across the room. When Johnny's eyes meets with his, he looks away, scratching his chest, acting natural. Johnny's rubber hands begin to shake.

"Yeah, this is correct," the woman says. "You were late on a couple of gravity bills, so the hospital had us take the money from your account."

If Johnny's facial expression could change it would now be one of rage. "I haven't used gravity in over two months."

"I'm sorry, sir," says the teller. "Whether you use the gravity or not, you still have to pay for it. You didn't have enough money in your account to cover your last bill, so now your account is overdrawn. You owe us 1,923 dollars."

The bratty boy creeps through the line toward Johnny.

"But I don't have that kind of money!"

"You will be charged a $50 overdraft fee every day until the amount is settled."

"What!" Johnny cries.

The boy is now only a foot behind Johnny.

"If you don't pay the full amount by the end of the month 90% of your wages will be garnished."

"But I don't even have a job!"

"Then you better start looking," the teller says, closing the folder. "Next in line please."

"But I didn't want the gravity anymore," Johnny shouts, holding up his bag. "I've been using my own gravity!"

The black woman pushes Johnny out of the way and gives her account information to the teller. Johnny pushes her back and says, "You need to reverse those charges and give me my money. Now!"

A smile widens on the little boy's face as he aims his toy plane at Johnny's butt.

"Get out of my way, balloon," the black lady shouts, pushing Johnny back.

"Yeah, get out of here, balloon," another person shouts.

"Give me my money," Johnny says.

The teller makes eye contact with the guards in the back of the room. "Sir, if you don't leave now security is going to escort you out."

"Give me my fucking money!"

The little boy raises his toy airplane.

Johnny puts his hand in his knapsack, feeling around the pieces of debris. The guards move in toward him.

"BOOOM!" the kid says, as the toy plane flies toward Johnny's back.

Before the toy pierces his skin, Johnny pulls out a .32 caliber revolver and shoves it in the kid's face.

"Get back or I'll blow your fucking face off, you little shit!"

When the kid sees the gun and Johnny's demented smiling face peering down at him, he drops the toy. Then he begins to cry.

The doors of the bank break open and four people enter wearing gasmasks and holding shotguns.

"Everyone down on the ground," one of them yells, while two others stab the barrels of their weapons into the backs of the security officers.

The four armed robbers wear matching gray latex body suits. One is a woman wearing a suit with red hearts printed onto the chest and shoulders. One man of average build has black spades on his suit. A very large muscular man has a suit patterned with black clovers. And the tall, curvy woman has a biohazard symbol printed across the skin-tight latex.

"Get down!" the robbers cry, pushing the customers to the ground.

The people in line behind Johnny slowly fall to their knees around him. They cower beneath his weapon as he points it around the room, trying to figure out what's going on.

Some people near Johnny—like the bank teller and the black lady—do not go down. They are still in shock that Johnny is pointing a gun at the boy. Sure it was okay for the kid to murder a few balloon people, but now that the tides are turned they start to show some concern. A kid popping balloon people is kind of cute to them, but a balloon man threatening a boy with a gun, that's appalling!

"You heard them," Johnny shouts at the people around him. "On the floor. Now."

Then everyone around the balloon man crouches down, lying flat on the floor. All of them except the teller. Johnny turns to her.

"Now… where were we?" He points the gun at the woman. "Oh, that's right. We were talking about *my* money."

The teller's white glasses slip down her nose, but she's too nervous to push them back up.

SAILBOAT

In the alley around the corner from Liberty Bank, Sailboat was struggling to pull on his latex outfit. It was a bit too small for the big oaf. The zipper wouldn't go up in the back. It was tight in the crotch. The clovers on his pectoral muscles made it look like he was wearing a black bra over his man-breasts.

"Are you paying attention, Sailboat?" the bald black man said to him. "I don't want any fuck ups."

"Yeah, I hear you."

The bald man pointed at Sailboat and the voluptuous Italian girl standing next to him. "You and Doomsday go for the two guards." He looks over at the thin woman with short red hair and glasses. "Nine and I will go for money. Remember, there will be an undercover guard in the bank somewhere. Keep an eye out for him."

"Got you," Sailboat said.

"Little Sister," the bald man said to the teenaged girl standing behind them. "The bags."

The girl brushed her blue dreadlocks out of her eyes and tossed him two duffel bags. The bald guy opened them and passed out the shotguns.

"I get the Tommy Gun," said Miss Doomsday, the Italian girl wearing the latex suit patterned with biohazard symbols. "You know I always get the *big* gun."

The leader handed her the Tommy Gun, then looked at his team. "Ready?"

They all nodded.

"Jack," Nine asked the bald guy. "You forgot one thing."

"What?" Jack asked.

She grabbed him around the neck and kissed him.

"For luck," she said, then sucked his tongue into her mouth.

His smile curled around her lips. She smiled back when she pulled away.

"Okay," he said. "Let's go."

They put the gas masks over their faces and held up their weapons.

As they headed out of the alley, Jack looked over to the teenager, "Keep your eyes peeled, Little Sister. We're counting on you."

She gave him the devil sign as she went toward her bike. "Good luck."

Just outside of the bank, they pumped their shotguns and gave each other a nod. Then they broke through the entrance and stormed the bank.

"Everyone down on the ground," Jack yelled, while Sailboat and Doomsday stabbed the barrels of their weapons into the backs of the security officers.

Taking out the guards was even easier than expected. They were standing right in front of the entrance, with their backs turned. It was going to be their lucky day.

Sailboat is a resident of Crab Town. He's lived there for quite a while now, in a charred cavern beneath a collapsed office building. Sailboat believes it is called Crab Town because of all the black sewer crabs that crawl through the streets. A lot of Crab Town residents catch these crabs in the bay or in the sewer, because they have nothing else to eat. But the crustaceans are poisonous and incredibly radioactive. You can live on them for a while, but eventually they're going to kill you.

Sailboat didn't always live in Crab Town. He had a pretty decent life growing up. But he's come across some hard times, like pretty much everyone since the United States became a third world country.

The reason why Sailboat moved to Crab Town was because he could no longer pay his debts. He had a steady job but his wages were garnished so much he couldn't afford his rent. He was forced to move to Crab Town and once he did that his employer fired him. Companies don't like to keep residents of Crab Town on their staff. They assume only deadbeats and druggies live on that part of town, even though over 70% of the citizens of Freedom City live in the Crab Town.

All of his bad luck has made Sailboat a very angry individual.

When Sailboat sees the guard going for his weapon, he clobbers him in the back of the head with the butt of his shotgun.

"Do you want me to hurt you, pig?" Sailboat screams down at him. "Is that what you want?"

He pulls the guard's gun out of the holster and tosses it away. Then he kicks him in the face and slams the butt of his gun down on the back of his head.

"Are you trying to kill him?" Doomsday screams over at him.

A pool of blood forms on the floor below the guard's face. He isn't moving anymore.

"Did you kill him?" Doomsday asks.

"I hope so," Sailboat says.

Sailboat is an asshole for good reason. His parents made him the way he is.

These days, parents don't take care of their children for free anymore. Kids are expensive. Parents can't just raise them and get nothing in return. So nowadays, parents charge their children for ever dollar they spend on them. Food, clothes, toys, rent, all of it gets added to their bill.

And once a child turns eighteen, parents expect them to start paying off their debt, with interest.

Unfortunately, the economy is a lot worse now than it was when Sailboat was a kid. Employers pay a lot less now than they did back then, and the cost of living has gone up. It's almost impossible for a kid to pay off the debt they owe to their family. Most of the time parents will let their kids slide, sometimes only asking they pay 5% of their earnings toward the debt. But not Sailboat's parents. They wanted their money. They didn't give a crap how bad the economy was. Sailboat's little brother already screwed them over by dying of a drug overdose at the age of nineteen, and they were going to be damned if their other son cheated them out of what they were owed.

And Sailboat owed them a lot, because they spoiled him as a kid. His parents had a rather large income. They had a large house, only ate the finest food, would only clothe their children with the finest designer wear, and always gave them tons of presents at birthdays and Christmas. But everything Sailboat got as a kid wasn't what *he* wanted, his parents gave him what *they* wanted. He couldn't pick out what food he ate or what he was allowed to wear. He might have been a little more thrifty if he'd understood how money worked when he was young.

His parents sent him to a very expensive art school that didn't really teach him anything useful. When he graduated, he didn't really have many skills to get a good job. He could hardly do basic math. His skills in painting and sculpture were pretty useless during these times.

He eventually got a job as a drywaller, but it was hardly enough to pay rent, let alone pay off his parents' debts. After he refused to pay their invoices, his parents got their lawyers involved. They managed to get his boss to garnish his wages, to give them half of his earnings. Sailboat begged his parents to take it easy on him, but they told him that *was* them being easy on him. They said they spent five times that amount on him per month, and that was just on his quarter of the house payments alone. Sailboat said he shouldn't have to pay a quarter of their mortgage if he wasn't a co-owner of the house, but they didn't care. Parents can charge their children whatever rent they want, even if they decide to rip them off. Kids are gullible and can easily be taken advantage of by parents who think ahead.

A part of Sailboat was actually happy that he was kicked out of his apartment and had to move to the Crab Town. He was happy because he was screwing over his parents and would no longer have to pay a single penny to those bastards. But he also knew that moving to Crab Town was the beginning of the end for him. He would never be able to get back on his feet for as long as he lives. If only his parents would have taken just 15% he would have been able to keep his job and pay rent. But they had to go and get greedy, even though they were still doing pretty well financially on their own. He will never forgive them screwing him like that.

Sailboat realizes that they've got an extra gun man working with them. He thought it was just the four of them and the teenaged girl outside. He isn't sure if the balloon man waving a .32 revolver at the bank teller is with them, or just some other guy robbing the bank at the same time. It's possible that he is with them. Sailboat never listens to Jack when he's given the game plan.

"Who the hell is that guy?" Sailboat asks Doomsday.

She looks over at Johnny Balloon.

"No idea."

"Is he with us?" Sailboat asks.

"No."

Since the security officer he should be guarding is out cold, or maybe dead, Sailboat leaves his position and goes to Jack.

"Put your hands on the back of your neck," Jack yells at the people on the floor. "With your face pointed at the ground."

Sailboat goes back-to-back with Jack and whispers behind his shoulder. "Who the hell is the balloon guy?"

Johnny Balloon hears and looks over at them. He locks eyes with Jack.

"You cool?" Jack asks the balloon.

Johnny nods. "I just want the money they owe me."

Jack looks over at Nine, then back at Johnny.

"Okay then," Jack says. "Get it and go."

Sailboat shoves his leader with his right shoulder. "You can't be serious."

"He's one of us," Jack says. "He's a crab."

"But we don't know him. And he's a fucking balloon."

"Yeah, he's a balloon. That's all I need to know about him to know he deserves a piece of this bank. He drew a worse lot in life than either you or I."

"He's going to get us killed."

"Let me worry about him. You worry about the third security officer. He's got to be here somewhere."

Sailboat grunts, then scans the quivering faces, looking for someone who doesn't belong.

"Are you guys looking for the undercover guard?" Johnny says.

The robbers all look at him.

"Try the guy with the yellow hat," Johnny says.

Jack nods to Sailboat, and the large man goes to the other side of the room. The man with the yellow hat grumbles to himself as Sailboat points his shotgun down at him.

"My right pocket," Yellow Hat says.

Sailboat pats him down and finds the handgun.

"It's him," Sailboat tells the others.

Jack smiles at Johnny Balloon.

"I told you," Jack says. "He's one of us."

Nine brings the bank manager and his wife into the front room and tosses them on the floor.

"Now that you're all here," Jack tells his captive audience, "I'd like to finally make an introduction." He raises his arms in the air and says, "We are the House of Cards." He presses his hands together and paces in front of the crowd. "Or at least four of the fifty-two members of the House of Cards. Maybe you've heard of us. I'm called Jack of Spades, one of the proud Lieutenants of our brave little army. The sexy lady next to me is the Nine of Hearts. She'll steal your soul given the chance. Over there we've got the Four of Clubs, or Sailboat, as we like to call him. And the girl with the big ass Tommy Gun is the lovely Miss Doomsday. Whatever you do, don't piss her off. She's one fine weapon of mass destruction."

He looks over at Johnny, "And who are you again?"

"They call me Johnny Balloon," Johnny replies.

"Ah, yes," Jack says, smiling behind his mask. "And joining us for the afternoon is our provisional wild card, my main man, Johnny Balloon."

The balloon man gives the hostages a squeaky bow.

"We're all from Crab Town," Jack continues. "That's right, the place a lot of you try to pretend doesn't exist. I can tell that some of you are residents of Crab Town, or on the verge of becoming residents of the shit hole. For the lot of you, I apologize for this inconvenience. Rest assured, your patience will be rewarded. As most of you know, the House of Cards doesn't commit crimes for our own financial gain. No, we do this for you, the little crabbies. All the money we make goes toward helping you crabs build a better life. We put money toward water filtration systems, so that we don't have to drink that toxic sludge that comes out of the sinks. We put money toward books to educate Crab Town children. We buy medicine. We buy food. We repair buildings.

We are your friends. We do this for you."

The guard in the yellow hat chuckles. "Yeah, you're a regular Robin Hood."

Sailboat stomps on his back for interrupting.

"Unfortunately, for the rest of you," Jack of Spades says to the guard, "you are not friends of the House of Cards. You have used us and thrown us away like garbage. Crab Town citizens aren't even allowed to get jobs because of you, because we disgust you. You don't want us working in your restaurants or factories. You won't even let us wash your floors. Are you afraid living out there in the impact zone has made us radioactive? Are you afraid we're going to track radiation onto your side of town? Are we biohazards? Or are we just too ugly and dirty for you to look at?"

He looks down at the bank manager's wife, who is lying on the ground with one arm around her little boy. She stares at Jack's boots as he peers down on her.

"The sad thing is," Jack continues, "we're not even asking you to care about us. You don't have to help us. You can be as self-absorbed as you want to be. We're just sick and tired of you doing everything you possibly can to keep us down, making absolutely sure we can never get back up again. You made us into bottom feeders, and you want us to stay bottom feeders. Until you give us a chance to work, give us a chance to pay back our debts without garnishing the majority of our wages, the House of Cards will continue to rob your banks and steal your wallets."

He nods at Doomsday. She steps away from the front door.

He continues, "Now, if you're a resident of Crab Town, you are free to leave. We don't want you mixed up in any of this."

The Crab Town citizens look around, then slowly begin to stand up.

Jack points his shotgun at a blonde woman as she gets to her feet. With her clean shirt and designer perfume, she's obviously not a Crab Town citizen.

"Crab Town citizens only," he tells her. "I've lived there

long enough to know the smell of a crabby. If you don't smell like one you don't get to leave."

About nine people get up and go for the door. Miss Doomsday escorts them out. One of them smiles at her as she leaves, and mouths a *thank you*.

Jack looks down at the bank manager and tosses him an empty duffel bag.

"Now if you can fill this for me we'll be on our way."

The bank manager looks up at him. Jack smiles behind his mask.

JACK OF
SPADES

Jack once had a wife and daughter. They led honest lives in a lower middleclass neighborhood. When the government proposed the idea of CRABs, Jack thought it was a great opportunity. He was a brilliant handyman, who could fix just about anything from plumbing to electrics to generators. His plan was to single-handedly renovate an apartment building in Crab Town, so that he could own the property and make a better living by renting apartments out to decent people. Then he would move on to another building and renovate that one, then another, and so on. He saw it as a way to get out of his dead end job and give his family a better life.

But things didn't work out the way he had intended. The buildings in Crab Town couldn't be renovated. It would be easier to tear them down and build new buildings from the ground up. But Jack tried to fix them. He tried to get at least one side of his building up to code enough to rent the apartments as low income housing. The city wouldn't approve, no matter how much money he sank into it. He could point out that some apartments on the more respectable side of town were in just as bad shape as this one, but the council wouldn't listen to him.

Later, he learned that the council had no intention of approving any of the buildings in Crab Town. The bill was passed just so they could get rid of the vagrants and lowlifes that infested the city streets, who no longer could contribute to society after the war. They just wanted to hide these people away so that they wouldn't have to worry about them anymore.

Jack lost his day job, but at the time he didn't realize it

was due to the fact that he was a Crab Town resident. A few months later, he heard stories from everyone in his neighborhood that they too had lost their jobs for no explainable reason. It was as if the government wanted to purposely keep them there, with the rest of the refuse. He believes that they don't call them Crab Towns for nothing. They call them that because it is where all the bottom feeders are sent. The people here are just radioactive scavengers, who eat everyone else's shit, just like the black crabs that come out of the sewers.

"Daddy, read me a story," his daughter asked him, lying in bed.

Jack smiled at her. "Of course, sweety. Which one?"

"The one about the prince and the garden."

"That's the one mommy has been teaching you to read, isn't it?"

She nodded.

"Then why don't you read it to me."

She shook her head.

"Why not?"

"I only know a few words. Mommy said she can't teach me anymore until she can see again."

Jack looked at the scar on his ring finger. The ring was stolen a long time ago, so the scar he received when it was ripped off is all that he has left to symbolize his love for her.

"What's wrong with her eyes, Daddy?"

Jack shook his head. "Don't worry about it, honey. She just needs glasses is all."

"She doesn't play with me much anymore either."

Jack brought the book to his daughter and sat next to her on the bed he had constructed out of particleboard and other scavenged wood. He pulled his feet out of the water puddle that covered most of his daughter's floor and lay down next to her. No matter how well he patched up the walls and ceilings, the water still managed to find its way in.

"Why don't we try to read it together," Jack said.

She nodded and laid her head on his shoulder. He kissed her on the bald spot in her hair.

"One day things will get better," he said. "Then you'll be able to go to a school. Eventually you'll be able to read stories to yourself."

She smiled up at him. "If I knew how to read I'd read every single day."

"Someday you will, honey. I promise someday you will."

Before the end of the year, both Jack's wife and daughter died of radiation poisoning. He isn't sure how they got it. When he still had an income, he paid inspectors who told him the water in the building was drinkable. He never fed them sewer crabs or any food that might have been con-taminated. But they both died nonetheless, leaving him all alone.

When he learned about a group of people trying to get organized in Crab Town, he signed up right away. At first, they were just trying to help out their fellow citizens. They fixed up buildings, organized gardening projects, set up a clinic, tried to convince companies to give their people work. Their deeds were somewhat successful, but it was never enough. That's when the organization took things in a more aggressive direction. They decided to become the House of Cards.

His real name was Oliver, but once in the House of Cards he became the Jack of Spades. Each Jack in the organization is responsible for a squad of soldiers, one from each suit.

The suits are divided up by specialty: spades are for those with book smarts, hearts are for those with street smarts and people skills, clubs are the muscle of the organization, and the diamonds are for the cunning and agile.

Jack immediately added the Six of Spades, aka Miss Doomsday, to his team. Her deceased husband, the King of Spades, was a close friend of his, so he knew she was the perfect choice for his team. But he had to recruit new people outside of the organization to fill his other three positions. Members of the House of Cards often get themselves killed, put in prison, disappear, or just plain quit, so there's always openings. There actually has never been a total of 52 members at one time since the organization began.

Sailboat was the second member he added to his team. Of all places, he found him out in the melt zone, where no one *ever* goes. The melt zone is where the bomb hit, leveling the entire area. Not a single structure was left standing. It's just a mile-wide crater of hot concrete slabs baking in the sun. It's the most radioactive area in town, so nobody steps foot there. The only thing you can find out there is an army of black crabs.

Some people say the melt zone is where all the sewer crabs come from. There are hundreds of them out there, crawling across the concrete, eating the red slime that grows in the acid rain puddles. Some of the crabs are enormous out there, the size of dogs or even bigger. They're vicious, too. You get too close to one of them and they'll take a chunk out of your thigh for breakfast.

Jack was out in the melt zone that day to drop off some money. He didn't trust banks and couldn't keep the money in his apartment or on his person. Muggings and break-ins are a weekly or daily occurrence in Crab Town. Even someone as tough as Jack could not protect his food and money. So he hid it out in the melt zone, where he knew nobody would ever go looking. It might eventually give him radiation sickness, but he didn't really care about that anymore. If death meant that he could be with his wife and little girl again he would welcome it.

After pocketing twenty dollars and returning his chest to its hiding spot beneath a flattened school bus, Jack heard someone shouting. He went deeper into the melt zone until he saw a muscular white guy running through the crater with a baseball bat, chasing after crabs. Jack assumed he was some crazed shitter.

A shitter is someone who gets high off of the drug called crab shit. It's not actually crab shit, but it is a mossy green substance that grows on the bellies of black sewer crabs. If you smoke it or consume it you're going to go on one hell of a trip. You'll go from euphoric to cosmic to violent to bat shit crazy all within the course of an hour. Then you'll need to do more. The stuff is radioactive and deadly as all hell, but most kids in Crab Town don't really give a fuck anymore. To them, just a tiny taste of happiness, even chemically-induced happiness, is worth dying for.

"Die bitches!" Sailboat yelled as he chased down a big black dog-sized crab.

Some of those bigger crabs aren't just the *size* of dogs, they can also run as *fast* as dogs. But they run sideways. Sailboat chased after it across slabs of sun-burnt asphalt. When he caught up to it, he broke two of its legs first, crippling it. Then he smashed down on its black shell until its sludgy guts were covering him.

There were hundreds of crabs crawling through the debris, all sizes. Most of them were deformed; some had extra pinchers, others had extra long legs, some shells were lumpy or lopsided, some were conjoined together into a black spidery mass. Sailboat went from crab to crab, stomping on the small ones, cracking open the big ones. If he slipped and fell, the crabs would turn on him, ganging up on him to get him while he's down. Crabs usually only go after the wounded or the dead, so whenever Sailboat's leg fell through a hole in the rubble they thought he was injured and no longer able to walk. Some of them would get him, claw slices into his arms and back. But once his leg was free, he would continue smashing them to a soupy pulp.

Then Jack realized Sailboat wasn't after crab shit. You only have to kill one crab to get enough crab shit to last several days. Sailboat was in the melt zone just so he could kill crabs. Jack smiled at the strange young man, fascinated by him. He just sat there and watched, to see how long the kid could keep it up.

But when Sailboat ran across a black plate the size of a basketball court, Jack realized he had to intervene.

"Get out of there!" Jack called.

Sailboat turned and looked up at him.

"Under your feet!" Jack pointed at the black ground beneath Sailboat. "Get off of there!"

But it was too late. The ground rumbled, knocking Sailboat on his ass. He found himself being lifted two stories out of the rubble. When he rolled off of the black shell and slammed down on a bed of concrete, he found himself looking up at a monster. It was one of the giant mutant crabs that are usually only found deep in the bay.

Jack pulled a repeater out of his coat and ran down into the crater, shooting at the massive crustacean to draw its attention. But Sailboat didn't use the opportunity to get away. Once the crab turned toward Jack, Sailboat attacked the thing with his bat. He swung at one of its legs as hard as he could, but the bat just bounced off. It was like trying to chop down an olive tree with a two-by-four.

The crab roared like an angry elephant as it went for Sailboat. A crane-like pincher came down on him, crashing through a brick wall above his head. The other pincher cut a charred Buick in half as Sailboat ran between its legs.

Jack aimed for its head and fired a few rounds, planting one of them in the soft spot above its mouth. The crab roared again, turning to Jack. It scuttled like a threshing machine up the hill, pulverizing the asphalt beneath its feet. Jack fired as it came closer, several hitting right in the thing's face, but it didn't slow it down. Then his gun clicked empty, just as it hovered over him with a claw snapping in his direction.

Jack turned to run, but his foot broke through a rusted sheet of metal, pinning him to the ground. As he tried to free himself, he could hear the pinchers thundering behind him, exploding against the earth below as the creature attacked.

By the time his foot was liberated, the crab was shrieking ferociously. Jack couldn't tell why the creature was thrashing and roaring, until he saw Sailboat standing on top of the crab's shell. The large man had climbed the crab's back and was now hacking at its head, using a jagged old stop sign like an axe. Green sludge sprayed from its face, its eyes mutilated on the stalks. When Sailboat used the pointed edge at the bottom of the sign's pole like a spear, piercing through its face deep into its brain matter, the crab dropped to the ground.

Jack rolled out of way, barely escaping the impact as it fell. Then he stared at the monster as its legs curled slowly against its abdomen.

When they were sure it was dead, Sailboat and Jack leaned against its mossy shell and caught their breath. Jack smiled over at the large white guy and shook his head at him.

He said, "Why the hell are you picking fights with crabs all the way out here in the melt zone?"

Sailboat looked over at him. "Crabs piss me off."

"You come all the way out to the melt zone just to take out your aggression on crustaceans?"

The big guy chuckled. "Maybe not."

Then he looked up at the red sun and wiped blood from his forehead. "As long as these sewer crabs are breeding out here, kids are going to be dying from doing too much crab shit. Maybe I figured somebody should do something about that."

"You were planning on bringing the crabs to extinction, single-handedly, one bat-swing at a time?"

"Something like that."

Jack laughed.

After a short pause, Jack asked, "Ever hear of the House of Cards?"

"Sure."

"How would you like to join?"

Sailboat shook his head. "I don't see myself as the revolutionary type."

"Neither did I, before I joined. We need to work together if we plan to ever get out of Crab Town. We need to show the rest of the world that we are human beings, who deserve respect and equal rights. No matter how much they want us to, we will not just lie down and die quietly in this toxic dump they've locked us in."

"If joining will get me out of this place and back on my feet, count me in."

"I can't promise you that, but I can say that you'll do more good for yourself and our people than killing crabs in the melt zone."

Sailboat snickered. "Well, if you put it that way... Okay, I'm in."

"Good. I need some muscle for my squad and I know you'll be perfect. Not many clubs in the House of Cards can say they've slain a monster crab before."

Jack pulled a card out of his pocket, the four of clubs, and held it up to him. "This is who you are from now on. This is your new name and rank."

"I'm a sailboat?"

Jack eyeballed him. "What do you mean?"

"There," the big guy pointed at the number four on the card. "It looks like a sailboat."

"It's a four. The four of clubs."

Jack handed him the card. The new recruit looked it over, then put it in his pants.

"I've always called them sailboats."

Jack laughed. "Well, then. I guess we'll have to call you the Sailboat of Clubs, then."

"Fine with me."

Jack stood up and held out his hand to his new friend.

"Welcome to the team, Sailboat."

After he had his Sailboat of Clubs, he recruited Little Sister, also known as the Two of Diamonds. Then he got the Nine of Hearts, his lover. When his team was formed, they became legendary in the House of Cards. A powerhouse quintet. One that has yet to be equaled within the organization.

"Now if you can fill this for me we'll be on our way."

The bank manager looks up at him. Jack smiles behind his mask.

With the duffel bag in his hands, the bank manager shakes his head. "I know you think this is helping your people, but you have to know you're only making things worse."

The bank manager stands up. His wife grabs him by the wrist, trying to keep him by her side, but he gently removes her fingers and with his eyes tells her he'll be just fine.

"Every time one of you revolutionaries steals money from the bank, it only makes it more difficult for our society to get back on its feet. The reason the living condition in Crab Town remains atrocious is because the government doesn't have the funds to give you the aid you need. But the more money you steal from the bank, the more money the government has to give to compensate, and the less money they have to spend on social reform."

"Social reform isn't what we're after. If we were just given the chance to work and make a living we wouldn't need a free handout from the government."

"But taking criminal action only turns the rest of society against Crab Town. You appear to be violent, dangerous thugs that should be locked away from civilization. Next thing they're going to do will be to build a wall around Crab Town and shut you all out for good."

"There's a much easier way for them to solve the Crab Town problem," Jack says. "All they need to do is listen."

Jack sends Nine into the back with the bank manager to fill the bags. When she returns her bags are very light, not even half full.

"That's it?" Sailboat asks, glaring at the sagging duffel bags.

"It's everything." Nine shrugs her shoulders.

"Bullshit," Sailboat says. "They're hiding it back there, somewhere. Let me go see."

Jack holds him back.

"Don't worry about it," Jack says. "We need to get out of here."

"But we went through all of this just for pocket change?"

"The cash wasn't the point of robbing the bank," Jack says. "Our real objective is all that matters."

The day before, all five of Jack's team were gathered in a burnt out pizza shack in Crab Town, sharing a cold can of beans and going over the plan. They used paint buckets as chairs and a piece of an old billboard as a table.

"So the point of robbing the bank isn't to get money?" Nine asked.

"The money is just an added bonus," Jack said.

"So what's the real plan then?"

"Can't tell you yet," he said. "I'll let you know when the time comes."

Little Sister had her bike on the table, the sail lying on the floor next to them. Her tiny hands were greasy from tightening bolts and screws. She was short and bony, but her flesh was knotty with muscle. When she looked up at Jack, her face lit up.

"Does the plan involve my bikes?" asked Little Sister. "Is that why you had me fix up these bikes for you?"

Jack's squad usually made their getaways on foot, but this time Jack had requested they do it on bikes. And when it comes to bicycles, Little Sister is the authority.

"Yeah, that's right," Jack said. "We'll need to be able to move quickly after we hit the bank."

"What's with the secrets?" Sailboat asked. "You've never needed to keep anything from us before."

"This time's different. If you knew what I had planned beforehand you would never want to go through with it."

Sailboat groans at him. "Great…"

"Trust me, if we want the world to hear us out then this is the best shot we've got. They're not going to be able to ignore us anymore after this."

"Can't you tell us anything?" Nine asked.

"All I can say is Miss Doomsday is the key."

Doomsday choked on her beans. "Me?"

"We can't do this without you."

The Italian girl didn't like the sound of that.

"It's a bad idea not letting us in on the plan," Sailboat said. "What if something happens to you? What then?"

Jack leaned back on his paint bucket. "Then I guess you'll just have to make sure nothing happens to me."

Jack of Spades opens one of the duffel bags.

"How much do they owe you?" he asks Johnny Balloon.

The balloon says, "Almost sixteen hundred, but fifteen hundred would be fine."

Jack tosses him some stacks of bills. "Take two thousand. Thanks for helping us out."

"You're giving him two thousand?" Sailboat goes for the balloon, but Jack gets between them. "That's probably half of the take."

"Forget about it, let's go." Jack pushes him away. Nine and Miss Doomsday go for the door.

Sailboat shakes his head, and goes back for Johnny Balloon. "I can't just give the money to a fucking balloon."

Johnny backs away.

Jack catches up to Sailboat and gets in front of him again. "What's gotten into you, man? This isn't the same Sailboat I used to know. This isn't the Sailboat who spent half his time in the melt zone, trying to exterminate sewer crabs for the sake of getting our people off of the shit."

"I'm still the same Sailboat. I just don't think we should waste money on a goddamn balloon when we've got real people back home in need of food and medicine."

"He's a living person, too."

"But he doesn't need food or medicine. He doesn't need money like we do."

"He gets what is owed to him and that's final," Jack says. "Now let's go."

The two men go for the door, but when they get halfway across the room Sailboat turns and runs for the balloon man. When Johnny sees him coming, he raises his revolver.

A gun shot rings through the room.

Jack looks down at the stream of red draining from the hole his chest. Sailboat turns around. The Jack of Spades opens his mouth to speak, to tell Sailboat something he really needs to know, but only blood spills through his lips.

SAM
SMITH

Sam watches as the leader of the bank robbers tosses the balloon man some stacks of bills.

"You're giving him two thousand?" the large robber says, going for the balloon. "That's probably half of the take." Then the leader gets between them.

As they argue amongst themselves, Sam decides it's time to make his move. The two female robbers have their weapons down, distracted by their friends' argument. If he's going to stop these people it's now or never.

He looks over at the bloody guard on the floor, who winks at him with his one open eye. The guard has been playing possum ever since the big guy clubbed him in the back of the head. Sam makes eye contact with the other undercover guard and he gives him a nod. It's lucky the criminals didn't know the bank upped its security a little. The new policy is to have two plain-clothed guards in the bank during banking hours.

Sam can't afford to let these scumbags get away with the cash. At this job, the security guards are held responsible for every dollar that is stolen from the bank. If the thieves get away with money that amount comes out of the guards' paychecks.

With all the robberies happening these days, Sam can't allow another criminal to get away. The bank was taking so much money out of his pay, due to all the successful robberies, that he could no longer afford rent and was kicked out on the streets. He now has to sleep on his ex-wife's couch, living with her new husband, Ron. He has to listen to them have sex in the next room every night, and has to bear watching his two-year-old daughter treat Ron like her real dad. His daughter thinks of Sam as some kind of stranger invading their home. She's even scared of him.

Sam only has one month until he pays off the bank for the last robbery. The only reason his ex-wife still lets him stay with her is because she knows she only has to endure it for one more month. If he fucks up here today he won't be getting paid for another six months, then she's going to kick him out on the streets. In a week he'll be living in Crab Town robbing banks himself.

When he looks over at the other guards, he can see it in their eyes. They can't afford to let these House of Cards assholes get away with the cash either. If they don't stop them they'll lose everything they have.

As the big guy goes for the balloon man, Sam pulls his handgun out of its holster on his chest, then pulls out the backup pistol from the holster on his ankle, keeping both guns beneath his coat. The wounded guard looks over at his handgun in the corner of the room. The other guard watches Miss Doomsday's Tommy Gun hovering above him.

When the security officer with the yellow hat nods at him, Sam places his backup pistol slowly on the ground. With his left hand shielded from the robbers' view, Yellow Hat's fingers signal a count down to his fellow guards.

3...2...

"He gets what is owed to him and that's final," says the Jack of Spades. "Now let's go."

1...

Sam slides the pistol across the floor to Yellow Hat and stands up. Johnny Balloon sees the guard aiming his gun at Jack. He raises his revolver, points it at him, but Sailboat gets in his line of fire.

Sam shoots a round, hitting Jack in the center of his chest. The other robbers freeze up. They watch as their leader falls to the ground.

A guard grabs Miss Doomsday's Tommy Gun and it fires wildly across the floor. The hostages scream and crawl for cover. When Sailboat jumps to the ground, dodging bullets coming at him from Yellow Hat's pistol, Johnny finally has a shot at Sam.

Johnny fires. The balloon man obviously has never fired a gun since his transformation, because he's not prepared for the kickback. The blast sends his balloon body flying into the air, spinning up toward the ceiling. The bullet misses the guard by seven feet.

Nine doesn't react or move from her position by the exit. She just stares at Jack's lifeless body. She can't believe her leader, her lover, is actually dead. She didn't even know it was possible for a man like that to die.

When she snaps out of it, she lowers the barrel of her shotgun to the guard grabbing Doomsday's Tommy Gun and blows his skull into a spaghetti-like mess.

Covered in gore, Miss Doomsday kicks the officer's corpse to the ground and fires her machine gun at the guards. She cuts down the other uniformed guard, splitting him in half at the waist, and the bullet-shower forces Sam Smith to leap over the bank counter to get cover.

A bullet grazes Sailboat's shoulder and he drops his shotgun.

"Mother fucker!" Sailboat says, clutching at his arm.

As Yellow Hat aims for the big guy's head, he doesn't see the Nine of Hearts coming up behind him. Nine pumps her shotgun and blows Yellow Hat's left leg in half at the kneecap. The security officer doesn't realize what's happened until he hits the ground and sees his shredded leg sliding across the tile floor. He's in so much shock he hardly feels a thing.

As Nine pumps again and aims for his head, Yellow Hat rolls over and fires two slugs into her belly. She squeezes the trigger as she falls. The guard's brain looks like scrambled eggs in red snot as they explode out the top of his hat.

When Sam peeks out from behind the counter, he sees his three fellow guards are all dead, but there's only one of the thieves still standing. He aims for Doomsday's chest as she reloads her Tommy Gun. If he takes her out he might still be able to prevent the robbers from getting away with the cash, even though he's the only guard left. But before Sam can fire, Johnny Balloon slams his knapsack full of concrete down on his forehead.

NINE OF
HEARTS

Sam goes out cold. His face slides down the counter and lands in the orange-haired teller's lap as she cowers under her work station.

When Johnny looks up, he sees all of the hostages making a run for the exit. Sailboat picks up his shotgun with his good arm and staggers toward the duffel bag of cash. Miss Doomsday is standing over Nine with her Tommy Gun pointed in the air.

"Fuckfuckfuck," Nine cries, rolling on the tile floor with her arms hugging tightly to her stomach wounds.

As she cries, she stares at Jack's body lying in the center of the room. She still can't believe he's dead. He meant everything to her. He's the only reason she joined the House of Cards in the first place.

Nine was never a very caring person. She only gave a damn about one thing. Herself. If somebody would have asked her to join the House of Cards a few years ago and she would have told them "What's in it for me?"

Ask her to risk her ass to help other people and she would just laugh at you until you walked away. But when Jack asked her, she wasn't laughing. She signed on as the Nine of Hearts without the slightest hesitation.

Nine used to run Crab Town's *radiation fetish* porn ring. After the last nuclear attack, a lot of people in the country developed a fetish for radiation. Nine couldn't explain why some people found radiation sexually stimulating. She's not

49

even sure the people who have the fetish understand it. But she did know that some people would pay a shit load of money to get their hands on masturbation material that could satisfy this urge.

Nine needed money. She worked in the corporate office of a printing company, but had been fired because she had an STD. These days, employers regularly enforce their ethics onto their employees. It started with drug testing. Then, employees were not allowed to smoke or drink alcohol, even outside of work in their free time. Now, employers have taken things in an even bigger direction. They require employees to attend church every week. And the latest trend is for employers to test for STDs, because they don't want sexually promiscuous employees representing their company.

When Nine tested positive for MC (molluscum contagiosum), she couldn't believe it. She didn't have any of the symptoms and she had not had sex with anyone since her first husband died three years prior. Yet there was no way around it, she definitely had the STD. When she went to the doctor, she learned that the virus can also be spread via toilet seats. In her apartment building, there was only one bathroom per floor that all the tenants shared, so she could have picked it up from anyone. Her company didn't believe her excuse, though. She lost her job and became no longer employable in Freedom City.

But Nine wasn't one to give up. If she couldn't find a company to employ her she would just start her own company. The first thing that popped into her head: radiation porn. She knew lots of people with the fetish and there wasn't anyone creating masturbation material for them. So Nine moved to Crab Town and started her own radiation fetish business. And it quickly became an empire.

Since radiation was intangible and couldn't actually be filmed, Nine instead filmed the effects of radiation. She would find beautiful, young, desperate, starving Crab Town residents, give them a warm place to live, feed them hot food and make sure they had a steady intake of crab shit. Once radiation sickness set in, she would film them having sex.

They were basically snuff films. Even though her "actors" would be able to make appearances in several films before they died, she was killing them on camera nonetheless. A slow, erotic, painful death. Then she would toss their bodies out in the melt zone to be eaten by crabs. Nine thought they called the place Crab Town because in the end everyone who dies in Crab Town eventually becomes food for the crabs.

The films that earned her a shit load of money were the ones shot just before her actors died. There were certain things her clients wanted to see, and one of the major ones was human skin sliding off appendages. One popular shot that she tried to get as much as possible was to have a man bite a woman's nipple, then slide the skin off of her breast in one large sheet.

Her clients also liked when teeth effortlessly fell out of the gums, so another popular shot was to get a close-up on a woman's mouth as the guy's erect cock casually knocked her teeth out. Once all of the teeth were gone, she would give him a blow job with her soft gums. The money shot was when the woman pulled the skin off of the man's dick as if he was wearing a rubber, then jerked his raw skinless penis until he shot cum into her face. It would be an added bonus if the cum had blood in it.

When the House of Cards decided they wanted to put an end to Nine's porn ring, they sent Jack to do the job. They told him to stop her, even if he had to kill her. But that's not Jack's way. He decided to try and reason with her.

Nine was immediately attracted to Jack the second she saw him. He had an arrogant confidence about him that she found so cute.

When he asked her, "Will you please shut down your business?" she almost squealed with delight.

He's so adorable, she thought, and gave him a big smile.

Of course, there was no way she was going to give up her business just because some cute guy asked her nicely. So she sent him off and admired his ass on its way out the door.

But Jack wasn't the kind of guy who would give up that easily, and Nine knew it. Even though she knew it was a waste, she sent her men out to have Jack killed. She couldn't let her lust get in the way of her business. However, her men couldn't kill him. Those who went after him wound up either dead or seriously wounded. There were even a few that Jack persuaded into joining the House of Cards.

This only made her more attracted to the Jack of Spades. The guy was a hero. Nine was turned on by heroes. And when he started hijacking her shipments, cutting off her connections to the outside world, it only drove her more crazy with desire.

The next time Jack paid Nine a visit, she was expecting him to bring an army of his House of Cards buddies. But it wasn't an attack. He came to ask her out on a date. The audacity of his proposal was too much for her to refuse.

Going on a date in Crab Town pretty much meant to go for a walk on the bay, which is what Jack had intended. But Nine wanted nothing to do with that. She took him out to eat at a nice downtown restaurant outside of Crab Town, spoiling him with mint cocktails and clam pasta. She even bought him some new clothes for the occasion, which made Jack feel a bit like a Ken doll.

"This is a shocking turn of events," Nine said. "Yesterday I was trying to have you killed and you were trying to put me out of business, today we're having a romantic dinner together."

Jack just smiled.

"You have yet to tell me why you asked me out on this date."

"As you said, I'm trying to put you out of business," Jack said, then he took a sip of white wine.

"And?"

"And…" Jack shrugged. "Dropping everything to go out on a date with me meant that, for at least today, you'd be out of business."

Nine laughed out loud. "So that's your scheme…"

"It worked, didn't it?"

"Your strategy worked brilliantly. But, you know, tomorrow it's business as usual."

"Not if we go on another date."

Nine laughed again. She took another sip of wine and looked him in the eyes.

"Tell you what," she said. "I'll make you deal. Every day you go out with me I'll shut my business down. No films will be shot, no movies will be sold, no actors will be recruited. I'll consider it a day off."

"You've got a deal," Jack said.

Nine had no idea that Jack would take the offer so seriously. He decided to go on a date with her every single day from that point on. Originally she wasn't actually serious about shutting her business down just because they went on a date, but she found herself honoring the agreement. The whole thing amused her so much she had to keep her end of the deal. She just wanted to see how far Jack was willing to go.

After a month had gone by, Nine wondered if it was all a game anymore. She definitely had serious feelings about him, and she believed he had serious feelings about her even though he always said he was only dating her to keep her business shut down.

"Why don't you join me?" Nine asked him. "You could be a partner in my company. You know how much I make? Twenty thousand a month, tax free. Half of that could be yours. You wouldn't even have to do any of the dirty work. You could just be my business associate and personal bodyguard. Think about it. I'm willing to share it with you 50/50. I'd never make that offer to anyone else."

"50/50 would be what? 10,000 a month?"

"Yeah."

"Too low."

"Too low? How much does the House of Cards pay you per month? Nothing? Well, I'm offering you 10,000 times as much."

"I wouldn't sell my soul for so cheap."

"Come on, you can live a life of luxury. So few people live in luxury these days."

"You live in Crab Town. What do you know about luxury? Your movie dungeon is probably the most scummy, toxic pit in town."

"But I'm able to go on vacation any time I want. Maybe you should come with me on vacation and see what I mean. I'll show you what you're missing."

Jack tapped his plate with his fork.

"What do you say?" she asked.

Jack agreed to go out of town with her for five days. They ate shellfish, swam in a radiation-free pool, they even made love a few times. Nine thought she had finally won him over, she had finally got the hero to come to her side. But on the morning of the sixth day, she woke to find him gone.

When she got back to Crab Town, she learned that her film studio had been burned to the ground. Her actors had fled and her workers were missing. She could no longer contact her distributors and clients, many of which had been imprisoned. And to top it off, her bank account was empty. Jack was behind it all.

"You probably could have convinced me to retire without robbing me blind," Nine said to the Jack of Spades, as she watched him hammering shingles onto a rooftop.

Jack continued hammering without even looking at her.

"I actually fell in love with you, you know," she said.

When he didn't respond, she grabbed his leg and pulled him off the ladder. He landed on his feet, right in front of her.

"I fell in love with you, too," he said.

"And so you screwed me over…"

"It had to be done at some point." He walked away, toward his toolbox. "I couldn't be in a serious relationship with anyone who profited from the misery of others."

She followed. "So that's it? You tear down my business, tear out my heart, and now you're just going to dump me?"

"How can I dump you? We were never a couple?"

"But you just said you were falling in love with me, too…"

"That doesn't mean I was your boyfriend." He turned to her. "Now that you've gone clean and donated all of your wealth to atone for your crimes, I'm willing to forget the past and start over. That is, if you'd like."

Nine sneered at him. "After what you did to me? You can't be serious."

"It's the first time I've ever considered actually getting serious with you since we've met."

Nine opened her mouth to speak, but hesitated. Jack pulled a card out of his pocket and held it in front of her face. It was the nine of hearts.

"I'd like you to join the House of Cards," Jack said.

Nine took the card.

Jack said, "My collaborators might not agree with me, but I think you would be excellent for the organization. Your business might have been morally appalling, but you were still able to create a successful empire out of nothing… and in Crab Town, of all places. If you were to use your skills to help the people, rather than just to help yourself, I think you could do great things."

Nine paused for a moment. Then burst into laughter.

"So you're seriously saying that you want me, a selfish murdering pornographer who's tried to have you killed on numerous occasions, to join the House of Cards?"

He nodded. "And continue dating, for real this time. If you're interested."

Nine could tell that he was actually serious.

She took a deep breath and said, "You're such an asshole." He smiled at her and she found herself blushing. "...I can't believe I'm saying this, but yeah. I'm in. I'll be your fucking Nine of Hearts."

And from that point on, Nine was a new woman. She was poor and hungry, but she was happy, truly happy for the first time in her life. She was also utterly, madly, desperately in love.

Tears flow down Nine's eyes as she looks at Jack's cold, peaceful face. She curses herself for not protecting him.

When she rolls her vision around the room, she sees Miss Doomsday standing over her. Most of the hostages have fled the building, except for a few still cowering in the corners. One lady is pressing on a bullet wound on her thigh. She must have gotten hit in the crossfire.

Sailboat is on the far side of the room, pointing his shotgun in the balloon man's permanently smiling face.

"You fucking shot him," Sailboat yells.

"It wasn't me," Johnny waves his rubber hands.

"I saw you. You were aiming at me, but you hit Jack."

"I was aiming at the guard," Johnny says. "If you didn't block my shot he wouldn't be dead now."

Sailboat pumped his shotgun. "You trying to blame this on me?"

"Enough," Doomsday says to them.

"But he shot Jack," Sailboat says.

Doomsday puts her Tommy Gun on her shoulder as she cat-walks over to them. "I saw it happen. A guard shot Jack. There was a second one in plain-clothes that we didn't know about."

Sailboat kicks his boot through the counter. He hears the bank manager gasp at the noise on the other side.

"We need to get out of here," Doomsday tells the others, as Sailboat goes around the counter to the bank manager.

"Not until he tells me where the rest of the money is." Sailboat picks up the scrawny man.

"You have all of it already," says the bank manager. "The vault's empty."

"I'll believe it when I see it."

When the bank manager originally opened the vault for Nine, she couldn't believe it either. The vault was practically empty.

"This is it?" she asked him.

The bank manager nodded. "You're disappointed. I completely understand."

"You completely understand!"

"Trust me, I'm even more unhappy to see it empty than you are. Filling a couple bags full of money for you wouldn't have been a setback at all for this bank, had you come just a few days ago."

"What happened?"

"The owners of Liberty Bank came yesterday and cleaned out the vault. The bank hasn't been doing very well this past year, so I guess the owners decided to take the money and run."

"The fat cats knocked off their own bank?"

The bank manager frowned. "Regrettably, that's exactly what they did. They stole everyone's money and took off, leaving only enough to keep the bank going for a few more days while they made their getaway."

Nine sighed and started packing up the measly leftovers. "Desperate times…"

"Desperate, indeed."

When Sailboat returns from the vault with the bank manager, he has an irritated look on his face but he's not accusing the scrawny guy of lying anymore.

"Help Nine up," Doomsday tells him. "Those escaped hostages surely called the cops now. They'll be arriving any minute." Sailboat nods and goes to the wounded girl.

Doomsday looks over at Johnny Balloon, who is cuffing the unconscious security officer behind the counter. "You should go. You don't want to be here when the cops show up."

Johnny gives her a thumbs up.

When Sailboat tries to pick up Nine, she mumbles, "We've got to carry out Jack's plan."

"He didn't tell us his plan." Sailboat says as he lifts her. The wounded woman has lost a lot of blood and can't stand on her own feet without assistance.

"We have to figure out what he wanted us to do," Nine says, her eyes rolling back and forward. "He said that Doomsday is the key."

Sailboat shakes his head. "Forget about it."

Doomsday looks over at them as she takes the bags of money from Sailboat and tosses them onto her shoulder. "No, maybe she's right. Maybe we can figure it out. He also said that he wouldn't tell us the plan because if we knew we would never want to go through with it. What could he possibly have in mind that we would never want to go through with?"

Sailboat assists Nine to the exit as she sways and staggers. "I have no idea. It could be anything."

"…that also requires me…" Doomsday mumbles, running it over in her head. Then she stops in her tracks. "No, it couldn't be that…"

"What?"

"The bomb. There's no way he wanted me to detonate the bomb…"

Sailboat isn't listening anymore.

She contemplates out loud, "How would a plan involving the bomb fit in with the plan of robbing the bank… There's no way."

They can hear the sound of police whistles coming from the distance.

Her eyes light up. "Unless…"

"Let's move!" Sailboat yells, as he pulls Nine through the door.

Miss Doomsday follows, her Tommy Gun leading the way.

LITTLE
SISTER

Outside the bank, Little Sister was acting as the lookout. This was the usual job for her. Being only fifteen years old, Jack didn't want her getting involved if shooting broke out. She wasn't even allowed to carry a gun.

Jack had told her that this time he was going to take longer than usual, so besides lookout Little Sister had to prevent people from entering the bank. She dressed in a police uniform, her blue dreadlocks hidden under a hat. After the others went into the bank, she set up a barricade and directed cyclists and pedestrians around the block.

It wasn't uncommon for teenagers to work for the police department. Instead of going to school, many children had to get jobs by the time they turned ten years old. Children under the age of eighteen would work just as many hours as adults, but they would get only a third of the pay (or sometimes even less). And they would usually be assigned the most tedious jobs available. A lot of traffic cops were teenagers, as well as factory workers, janitors, dishwashers, even construction workers. Once child laborers turn eighteen they might be considered for fulltime positions, but more often than not their employers just fire them and hire a younger kid so that they don't have to pay them adult wages.

Little Sister was born and raised in Crab Town, so she has never had to work as a child laborer. But she can pull off posing as a child police officer well enough. As she directs cyclists away from the bank, nobody thinks twice about it. They see this kind of thing everyday. Even another police officer walking by her barricade didn't suspect a thing.

"Damn road work again?" the cop asked Little Sister.

She just shrugged at him and waved him on.

"Why do they even bother?"

When the cop saw a blue dreadlock pop out of her police hat, the man gave her a disapproving glance but didn't think anything of it.

Little Sister has always been smooth and confident. She knows how to act natural in any circumstance. Her motto is: *just act like you own the place and nobody will question you.* Even as a punk kid with dreadlocks, none of the passersby ever questioned her legitimacy.

The only time Little Sister lost her poise was when she heard the gun shots coming from inside the bank. It happened while an old woman was bugging her to let her through the barricade, unwilling to take the detour.

"Just let me through," said the lady, holding two brown grocery bags full of meats and cereals. "I just need to go two blocks down."

"There's been a radiation spill in the area, ma'am," said Little Sister. "It's for your own safety."

"I'm old. Walking the long way around would be more damaging than a little radiation. I made it through two nuclear blasts, so I think I can make it through a little spill."

"I can't make an exception, not for anyone," said Little Sister. "If I let you through I could lose my job."

"You could lose your job if you *don't* let me through," said the old lady. "I'll let the police department know that you mistreated an old lady. I have friends in high places around here. You'll be out of the job."

"Make a complaint if you must, but you are not getting through. Please move along."

The old lady pulled out a pen and ripped off a piece of a grocery bag to write on. "What is your name?"

"Junior Officer Samantha Kensington."

"What is your boss's name?"

"John…"

Then the gun shots rang out in the bank. Little Sister was taken aback. She looked around, she didn't know what to do.

"What was that?" the old lady asked.

"It… It was nothing. Don't worry about it."

But the old lady wasn't talking about the gun shots.

"I asked you your boss's name, missy!"

"Oh… Captain John Dearmother."

She could hear the Tommy Gun roaring through the bank. It seemed the old lady was too hard of hearing to notice. Or perhaps she just didn't care.

"Dearmother?" asked the old lady.

Little Sister realized the name was a little too fake, but she was caught off guard and that was what spilled out.

"I'll make sure you are fired by the end of the week," said the old woman, finally moving on her way. "That will teach you for not helping an old woman in need."

Soon after that, people were running out of the bank, spilling into the street toward her. Even these people didn't catch on she wasn't a real cop.

"They're robbing the bank!" one of them said. "Call for backup. Two cops were already shot."

One man was even ready to give a full report to her. he said, "The robbers were two women, two men, and a balloon. They called themselves the House of Cards and wore gas masks. I can't tell what they looked like beneath the masks, but I can give you their builds and hair color."

"That won't be necessary," Little Sister told him. "Just go home, get out of the street. You're not safe here."

The man agreed and took off running.

Little Sister tossed her police hat and went for the bikes in the alley. She raised their sails and pointed them into the wind. When she heard the police whistles, she wasn't sure what to do. Jack had told her not to enter the bank if she heard gun shots. She was instructed to wait three minutes and if they didn't come out, she was supposed to get out of there on her own.

She waited three minutes, then got on her bike. The police whistles were getting closer. She couldn't be seen in her fake uniform.

When her colleagues left the bank, she could tell the job went wrong. Horribly wrong. Two of them were wounded and Jack was nowhere to be seen.

"Where is he?" Little Sister asks as they come into the alley.

"Jack's dead," says Doomsday, helping Nine onto the back of Sailboat's bike.

"What?" Little Sister giggles nervously at the thought. "He can't be…"

"He's fucking dead!" Sailboat yells at her.

Little Sister flinches at his words.

They see Johnny Balloon running past the alley, with gunshots trailing behind him. The cops have arrived on the scene and have already opened fire on the first guy they see carrying a gun. Bullets whiz past his head. He screams in a panic, knowing that he'll pop at the slightest graze.

"We've got to save him," says Miss Doomsday.

"Leave him," says Sailboat. "We'll be able to get away as he draws the fire."

"I'm going for him," Doomsday says.

"But you don't even know him."

"Let's split up. Meet back in Crab Town, in the square."

"You can't be serious. He's a fucking balloon!"

As she dismisses him and peddles out into the street, Sailboat kicks the wall. Going after her would be stupid, especially with Nine to look after. The Nine of Hearts is sitting on the bike, shivering from the loss of blood. He can't worry about Doomsday right now. He has to get Nine back to Crab Town, to the doctor, the Queen of Spades.

As Sailboat gets on the back of the bike with Nine,

Little Sister passes him, peddling into the street after Miss Doomsday.

"Where are you going?" he yells.

"She needs me." Little Sister doesn't look back. "I'm the Two of Diamonds. Escaping from the police is my department."

The big guy doesn't argue. He looks down at Nine and peddles off, in the other direction.

When Little Sister enters the street, the cops stop firing. They see a teenager in a police uniform and think she's on their side for a brief moment, until she rides up next to Miss Doomsday with a matching bike.

Little Sister was the leader of one of Crab Town's most violent street gangs, *The King Crabs*. Being a kid in Crab Town with dead parents you have pretty much only one option if you want to survive: you join a gang. And once you're in a gang, it's kill or be killed.

The King Crabs were a bicycle gang that claimed about forty percent of Crab Town, including the House of Cards' area of operation. Now that gas-powered vehicles are as rare as clean water, most people use either pedal-powered or sail-powered transportation. The King Crabs use both. They created sail-bikes, which are kind of like a combination of sailboard and BMX bike. Little Sister was building them since she could walk and by the time she was old enough to crack a shitter's head open with a brick, she had a gang of street warriors riding her sail-bikes and taking her commands.

On their sail-bikes, the King Crabs are the fastest people on the road. Not even the cops in their giant street boats can catch them. They ride onto their enemy turf with spears and axes, slicing through them and sailing away before they know what hit them. Although they are not the biggest gang in Crab Town, they are the most dangerous, and most feared.

The King Crabs and other Crab Town gangs have a different kind of existence than anyone else in the city. They aren't interested in rebuilding or returning to civilization. Instead, they embrace the wasteland. They live like road warriors of the post-apocalypse out in the ruins. Only, instead of vehicles, they use wind-powered bicycles. Instead of guns, they use javelins and arrows. They are returning to a more primitive, tribal life. And anyone who isn't one of them is considered their enemy.

The House of Cards decided they had to do something about these punks causing havoc in Crab Town. After shutting down the radiation porn ring, the House of Cards thought Jack would be the right person for the job. But he wasn't. Jack had a respect for the King Crabs. Instead of getting rid of them, Jack wanted to join forces with them. He thought they were well-organized and damn near invincible. If only their moral compass was in the right place.

The first time Jack tried to communicate with the King Crabs, they beat him nearly to death with bike chains. He explained that they were on the same side, that Crab Town citizens were their family, and that they should work together against the fat cats of Freedom City.

"Someday you won't have to live like wild animals anymore," Jack said.

It was the wrong thing for him to say.

"We *want* to live like wild animals," said Little Sister. "The rest of you live like sick, dying, caged animals. At least we're free."

"If we work together we can have a better life," Jack said.

But these kids have never known the old world. They grew up in Crab Town. They only know two ways of living: hard and fast or waiting to die. They love living like wild animals in the ruins of Crab Town, taking whatever they want, doing crab shit, and waging war against rival gangs. They thought the place was called Crab Town because the

King Crabs owned it.

Jack couldn't get through to them. But he wouldn't give up. They beat him bloody, but once his wounds healed he came right back. Then they beat him again.

The fourth time Jack visited them, one of the younger kids in the King Crabs gang was suffering from a head wound after crashing into a brick wall while high on crab shit. The kid was jerking on the ground, hemorrhaging blood, part of his skull broken wide open. Jack tried to go to the boy, to see if he could help, but Little Sister's friends got in his way.

"Don't touch him," Little Sister said, two of the bigger kids were at her side.

"I have a friend who could help him," Jack said. "If we get him to her she might be able to save his life."

"A King Crab doesn't need help from anybody," she said. "If he's tough he'll survive on his own. If he's weak he deserves to die."

"So you're just going to sit around and watch him die?"

"It's our way," she said.

"Bullshit," Jack said. "It's a waste."

Jack tried to go for the boy, but the King Crabs held him back. They punched him in the stomach, then knocked him to the ground. They took out lead pipes and threatened to beat him worse than the previous beatings combined.

"Let him go," Little Sister said, before they could break his face.

The others were surprised at her mercy.

"I'm sick of looking at his face. Get him out of here."

While he was being dragged away, Jack made eye contact with Little Sister. He could tell she was confused by him. Nobody had ever offered to help a King Crab before. She thought the rule of Crab Town was that you only look out for yourself. Part of her was angry that Jack offered to help. He was breaking the rules of the land by doing that. He was offering the kind of compassion and aid that she had been longing for as a child after her parents died of radiation sickness. She was always wishing somebody would help her find food or give her medicine or help her build shelter, but nobody ever gave a shit about her. She resented him for showing compassion. She hated him for it. But she showed him mercy. There was a part of her, deep down inside, that was grateful to him. Even though she couldn't allow him to actually save the kid and destroy their way of life, she was grateful that someone actually cared enough to try.

Two weeks later, the tables were turned. It wasn't Jack who came to the King Crabs. Little Sister had come to him. He woke to find her standing in his doorway, holding her stomach, bleeding on the floor. She was weak and could barely speak. During a gang fight, Little Sister had been stabbed in the stomach. Her friends wouldn't help her. They left her to die. She didn't know what else to do. She came looking for Jack.

The Jack of Spades was surprised she was able to track him down, figure out his location in the middle of the night, with a six-inch gash in her guts.

All she said was, "Help me," before collapsing onto the floor.

Jack scooped her up and took her to the Crab Town clinic run by the Queen of Spades. The clinic was a grubby old hospital that was falling apart worse than any other building in the area, but it was the best Crab Town had.

When Jack entered the lobby, the place was littered with balloon people floating in the air, their strings attached to the floor. They stuck around the clinic, hoping the impossible hope that someday the Queen might be able to restore them to human form.

"What happened?" the Queen asked Jack as she looked at him with bloodshot eyes. She always had bloodshot eyes from lack of sleep and nourishment. She was so focused on helping other people that she never had time to take care of herself.

"Stab wound," Jack said, putting her on an operating table. "She's lost a lot of blood."

"I'll see what I can do," said the Queen, getting straight to work.

Queen was a doctor who quit her job at the hospital in downtown Freedom City. She was morally opposed to how the hospital was treating patients. They only cared about making money off of the sick and wounded, and cared very little about helping them. The balloon people scam was one reason why she had to quit. It was a way for them to get free organ donation and then charge the rich out their ass for their desperately needed transplants. The hospital also regularly diagnosed their patients with bogus ailments in order to give them expensive, unnecessary operations. Many of these operations only harmed the patients and sometimes they would have to return to the hospital a week later to fix the damage the doctors had done. Then they would prescribe them expensive medication that they didn't even need, promising them that they risk serious health issues, including death, if they don't take the pills regularly, for the rest of their lives.

The Queen and a couple of her colleagues quit the hospital and set up the clinic in Crab Town, using her own savings to help the unfortunate people living there. She offered her services for free, but it only took a couple of weeks before her lack of funding prevented her from helping most of the patients who came to her. It wasn't until she joined the House of Cards, who donated a large percentage of their earnings to her cause, that the clinic actually became operational enough to help the Crab Town citizens. But it was never enough. People still died in her care everyday.

Jack was praying that Little Sister wouldn't be one of the unlucky patients that day. As Queen gave her blood (most of which she knew was radioactive) and closed up the wound, he watched Little Sister gazing up at the balloon people hovering above her as if they were angels coming to take her away.

When there was nothing else Queen could do, she said, "As long as she can fight the infection, she's going to pull through."

Jack was relieved.

When Little Sister awoke near dawn, she was surprised to see Jack standing above her. For a second, she had forgot what had happened. But once she tried to stand up and cringed at the wound, she remembered.

"You're going to be alright," Jack said.

She wouldn't look him in the eyes. After a long silence, Little Sister said, "You made a mistake."

"What mistake?"

"You should have let me die."

"You would prefer to be dead?"

Little Sister squeezed her fist open and closed. "I might as well be dead. By asking for your help, the King Crabs will never take me back. They'll think I'm too weak."

"Weren't you their leader? Don't you tell them what is weak and what isn't? Maybe all of you should change the way you think."

She shook her head. "They surely already chose a new leader. If I went back to them, the new leader would treat me as an enemy and a traitor." She was almost crying with her words. She had to pause for a moment in order to compose herself. "Without the King Crabs, I'm not going to last long. I'll be dead by the end of the month."

Jack handed her a card, the two of diamonds. "Not necessarily."

She took the two of diamonds.

"Join the House of Cards," he said. "You'll get a new lease on life. And maybe, one day, we'll create a better life for the people of Crab Town."

Little Sister joined. At first, she did because she didn't have anywhere else to go, but she quickly grew to love the job. She hated being treated like a kid by the rest of the Cards, but she had a lot of fun robbing banks and breaking into the homes of the rich.

Because she was the expert on building/repairing sail-bikes, the King Crabs eventually lost their advantage over other gangs. When they found out Little Sister was still alive, they tried to get her back. They didn't care that she had betrayed their rules. But she refused them. She had a better life with the House of Cards. Once her old gang threatened to kill her if she didn't go back to them, she had the King of Clubs and his thug-like army take them all out. Now the only people using sail-bikes in Crab Town are the House of Cards.

Little Sister is a master of the sail-bike. As the police charge after them on their tandem bikes, they have no way of catching up to her. She peddles fast and can take turns even faster. There are four tandem bikes coming after Doomsday and Little Sister. Each of them have a driver at the front of the bike, with a shooter in the back of the bike firing over their partner's head.

Miss Doomsday pedals up to Johnny Balloon as he runs through the street.

"Break off," she tells him. "We'll lead them away from you."

Johnny nods his head, but before he can turn into an alleyway, his knapsack breaks. The pieces of concrete weighing him down spill out into the street and Johnny loses his gravity. He floats up into the air, thrashing his limbs, crying for help.

Miss Doomsday goes for his string, but it slips through

her fingers. The wind blows him up the street, completely out of her reach.

"Help!" Johnny screams as he goes tumbling through the air, but there's nothing Doomsday can do to catch him.

Johnny points his revolver in the sky above him and fires, sending him back toward the ground. Doomsday tries to speed up to catch his string, but before she can reach he floats back up into the air. He fires again.

The cops assume that Johnny is aiming at them, and focus their gunfire at him instead of the robbers on the bikes. Instead of going for his string, Doomsday has to return fire with her Tommy Gun. She shreds the tires of one of the tandem bikes, sending the cops into the sidewalk. By the time Doomsday turns around, a gust of wind sends Johnny further up the road.

"I'll get him!" says Little Sister, blowing past Doomsday at top speed.

Miss Doomsday lays down some cover fire, as Little Sister sails through the street toward Johnny. Citizens try to run out of the way, getting caught up in the gun fight. Little Sister weaves through them effortlessly, trying to catch up to the balloon man before it's too late. He goes further down the street, higher and higher up into the sky.

Little Sister leaves the street and jumps over a row of steps, entering a building, she crosses the lobby of a dilapidated hotel, riding up the handicap ramp to the second floor. She rides to the back of the building, knocking hotel guests aside, then jumps from the balcony to the balcony on the other side of the street. Pedaling up to the rooftop, she sees Johnny at face level flying over the street beside her.

Keeping up with him, Little Sister jumps from rooftop to rooftop, sailing over alleys. Little Sister has been doing these kinds of stunts ever since she could ride, and knows these rooftops well. She set up half the ramps enabling her to make the jumps over the alleys. As a thief, she's created escape routes for herself that the cops could never possibly follow. She's had no problems losing the cops in the past and getting back to Crab Town without a trace. But she never thought she'd be using these rooftops to save a balloon man from floating away.

At the end of the block, the buildings end at a busy intersection. Little Sister has to make her move now if she ever wants to save Johnny. She takes a jump, into the street toward the balloon man. Just as she leaps a gust of wind hits, launching her sail further up into the air, but the wind also sends Johnny higher. She catches the last inch of string and pulls, wrapping the string around her handle bar. Then the two of them descend into the street.

Little Sister hits down hard, but she doesn't fall. Johnny Balloon looks down, amazed that the girl actually caught him up there. But when she doesn't pull him down, realizing he'll be stuck up in the air for the rest of the escape, he panics at the thought of how vulnerable he'll be... there are a lot of sharp objects he could slam into, not to mention he's an easy shot for the cops up there.

The second Little Sister enters the intersection, she's cut off by an enormous police street boat.

Because the police don't have the funding for gas-powered cars—only the most wealthy citizens can get their hands on fossil fuels—the cops use either tandem bikes or sometime they call in the street ships. With a dozen cops pedaling inside, it is a ship-sized bicycle with armor plating. The cops within fire at Little Sister through tiny windows as they pedal toward her.

Little Sister whips around the ship as bullets pass through her sail. The street boat might be large and armored like a bicycle-powered tank, but it still can't keep up with Little Sister's sail-bike. She takes a path through the alley, one that the boat can't get through, and forces the tank-like vehicle to turn itself around to go after her.

Miss Doomsday showers the windows of the street boat with a blast from her Tommy Gun, as she catches up to Little Sister. The street ship turns furiously around to go after them, slamming into a police tandem bike that was on Doomsday's trail. While parasailing through the air, Johnny fires the last of his bullets down on the police to cover the girls' backs as they make their escape.

"Follow me," Little Sister tells Doomsday. "I can lose them."

Doomsday shakes her head. "I don't want to lose them. We need to lead them to Crab Town."

"Why the hell would we do that?"

"I think this was Jack's plan," Doomsday says. "We want them to follow us."

Little Sister doesn't understand it, but she nods anyway. They speed up, out of the range of fire, but make sure the cops follow them all the way into Crab Town.

MISS
DOOMSDAY

Miss Doomsday always thought they called it Crab Town because in the middle of Crab Town, in the center of the old town square, there sits a 200 megaton Crab-Bomb that never detonated.

During the war, Crab Bombs weren't dropped by airplane. They were launched via submarine, and had six mechanical legs attached to them that crawled out of the ocean across the land, into the center of a city before detonating. But the bomb standing in the middle of Crab Town was one that never detonated. Somehow, when it got to its location, it never went off. It just stood there. The citizens in the area cleared out, they thought it would go off at any minute. But after a day, it was still standing. Then a week went by, then years, still fully capable of taking out the city, but it never happened.

The city wanted to disarm the device, but every specialist they sent in to do the job was too worried they would set off the bomb. They said even if it were moved the thing would detonate. So they just left it where it was. At first, they had soldiers guarding the bomb so that nobody would mess with it, but eventually the guards pulled out. The city council decided to ignore it, forget about it. But the bomb still stands in the center of Crab Town, ready to explode at any given moment.

Miss Doomsday's husband was the King of Spades. He was the last of the specialists who was sent in to disarm the bomb. But unlike the previous specialists, he wouldn't give up. Even after they cut his funding, even after he lost his job with the military, he wouldn't give up on the bomb. He became a permanent citizen of Crab Town and married his assistant, a young Italian girl with long raven-black hair. They became known as Mr. and Mrs. Doomsday, because most people believed they would one day blow up the entire city.

Being two of the few educated people in Crab Town, they were recruited into the House of Cards. The King of Spades spent a lot of his time helping the Queen of Spades with radiation treatments at the clinic. Her job was to help treat the radiation, whereas his job was to help prevent it. He tested which areas of town were the most radioactive and set up warning signs to keep people out. He taught the citizens how to protect themselves from radiation poisoning and how to survive in case the Crab-Bomb was ever set off.

But in his free time, he worked on figuring out a way to disarm the bomb. All he cared about was saving the city from another explosion. The government had abandoned the project. It was all up to him. But he never succeeded. Before he could finish his work, he was dead and gone. His wife changed her name to *Miss* Doomsday, and the House of Cards lost their most brilliant member.

When Miss Doomsday and Little Sister lead the police through Crab Town to the town square, Sailboat is waiting for them with a look of shock on his face.

"What the hell?" he says.

"This was Jack's plan," she tells him, jumping from her sail-bike. "The point of robbing the bank wasn't to get the money. It was to lead the cops here. To the bomb."

"Lead them to the bomb?"

"We're going to take the entire city hostage," she says, removing the gas mask from her face brushing her long black hair behind her shoulders. "This is how we are going to get those assholes to finally listen to us."

"That's what Jack had in mind?" Sailboat says. "Are you sure? The Four Aces would never approve of this."

Miss Doomsday doesn't reply. In all honesty, she knows she could be wrong and Jack could have had a completely different plan in mind. This plan sounds crazy, not at all something Jack would want them to do. But it is the only thing she could think of that would require Miss Doomsday, robbing a bank, and would be something that none of them would want to have anything to do with. The only way Jack could have gotten them to go with this plan would be to spring it on them when it was already too late to back out.

Little Sister brings Johnny back to his feet as the police close in on them, surrounding the area.

"Where's Nine?" Doomsday asks.

"Inside," says Sailboat.

"Let's get in there," Doomsday says. "We need to fortify the place. It's going to be a long day."

The King of Spades wasn't able to disarm the bomb, but he was able to protect it from crazy people who might decide to blow it up. He built a structure around it, a fortress that only members of the House of Cards could enter and leave. He also built a steel cage around the bomb that only himself and Miss Doomsday had the key to. If anybody outside of Miss Doomsday wanted to blow up the Crab-Bomb, they would have a hell of a time of it.

When they enter the fort, Sailboat locks the gate behind them. The cops surround the building.

"We need lookouts upstairs on all sides," Doomsday says. "I'll meet you up there in a minute."

Sailboat, Little Sister, and Johnny Balloon agree and charge up the stairs. Miss Doomsday goes into the back room to check on the Nine of Hearts.

"Are you okay?" she asks the woman lying on the concrete floor with a bloody pillow against her stomach.

"I'm losing feeling in my legs," Nine says.

"We'll get you to the Queen of Spades as soon as we can," says Doomsday, strapping the Thompson Gun to her back with an old cowboy belt. "Just hang in there."

Nine just blinks at the ceiling.

"Don't worry," Doomsday says. "I figured out what Jack wanted us to do. He's not going to have died in vain."

"You know Jack's plan?"

Doomsday nods. "I believe so. There will be no way they'll be able to ignore us after this."

Nine smiles. "I knew Jack would do it. I knew someday he'd have a plan that would save us all."

Doomsday watches her head swaying back against the wall, then decides she doesn't have the time to worry about her dying friend anymore. On the way out of the storage room, Miss Doomsday steps on a black crab crawling out of the storm drain, crushing it beneath her leather combat boot.

Then she goes into the central room, opens up the steel cage, and takes a look at the enormous Crab-Bomb. She cat-walks toward it, rubbing her finger along the metal casing. A radioactive gas pours out of the bomb and encircles her. She rubs her body as the gas surrounds her, breathing it into her body.

"We're going to save the world together, my love," she tells the bomb, rubbing her breasts through her latex radiation suit, purring within the glowing gas.

A lot of people in the House of Cards believe that Miss Doomsday is in love with the Crab-Bomb. Ever since her husband died, she started acting a little strange. She seemed to get lonely, eccentric, and then she started making love to the bomb.

They say that every once in a while a House of Cards

member will go to the bomb fort, and find Miss Doomsday naked on top of the bomb, straddling its casing. They'd hear her moaning, masturbating against the bomb, while surrounded by a radioactive gas.

But what they didn't know was that Miss Doomsday wasn't in love with the bomb, she was still in love with her husband. The reason she would masturbate on top of the Crab Bomb was because it was the closest thing she had to having sex with her husband.

The thing is, Miss Doomsday's husband didn't die. He was living in gaseous form. Like Johnny Balloon, the King of Spades went through the same operation in order to sell his organs and make money for the equipment he needed to finally disarm the bomb and safely transport it out of the city. Miss Doomsday was angry that he had the operation without consulting her, but he assumed the operation was reversible. She thought it would ruin their marriage, she thought she could never love a balloon, but she to accept it and try to make their marriage work.

The first time she made love to her balloon husband, Miss Doomsday popped him. When she came against his rubber body, she put too much pressure on his balloon penis, squeezing it tightly with her vaginal muscles until it popped. His entire body deflated beneath her. There was no longer life behind his expressionless face painted on the limp balloon.

Most of the time, when a balloon person pops their sentient gas rises and dissipates in the atmosphere. But when her husband died, Miss Doomsday believed his gas did not rise. His gas stayed with the Crab-Bomb. From that point on, she continued to make love with her husband against the bomb, in the only way she knew how. When she told her husband's closest friend, the Jack of Spades, that the gas flowing from the bomb was really her husband he believed she had gone crazy. He told her that the gas wasn't her husband and that she should stay away from it. But she didn't believe him. It was all she had left to remember him by.

When Miss Doomsday went upstairs, Sailboat was in the middle of a gunfight with the rest of the cops. He was firing his shotgun from the window, even though the cops were too far out of range.

"Get down," she tells Sailboat, crouching next to Johnny and Little Sister. "We don't want to fight them. We just want to talk."

Sailboat gets down and looks over at her. "They started shooting at me first. It's like they don't give a shit that we have a bomb big enough to blow up the entire city."

"They probably don't realize we've got it," she says. "It's been ages since Freedom City even acknowledged the bomb's existence."

Sailboat lets her take over.

She goes to the window, taking cover behind the wall, and shouts down to the police. "Stop shooting. We've got the Crab-Bomb in here. It's still fully operational."

Miss Doomsday has to repeat herself several times before they listen. The police cease their fire. A senior officer probably had to verify the story before they would believe her.

"It'll take less than one minute to detonate this thing," says Miss Doomsday. "It has the power to level the entire city."

The police remain silent. Several reinforcements come into the area every minute.

"I don't want to detonate the bomb if I don't have to," she says. "All I want to do is talk."

The police seem too busy ordering each other around, getting all of their men in key points around the building. After there are over a hundred men outside, they finally decide to speak.

In a megaphone, an officer calls out, "We have the place surrounded. Surrender now and you won't get hurt."

"Listen to what I'm saying," shouts Miss Doomsday.

"There is a Crab-Bomb in this place. Talk to the Mayor. He'll confirm this information. He surely knows that the bomb can still be detonated."

The cops don't respond for a while. Sailboat watches them through a crack in the wall. The cops in charge seem to be arguing with each other. One cop is furious with the cop in charge, yelling at him and pacing back and forth. The cop in charge isn't listening to him. He pulls rank.

The ranking officer says into the megaphone, "You've got five minutes to leave the building or I'm sending my men in there after you."

Miss Doomsday punches the wall.

"If you approach this building we *will* detonate the bomb," says Miss Doomsday. "We're not asking for money. All we want is to talk. You can at least hear us out."

The cops argue amongst themselves.

"Go ahead, talk," says the cop in charge.

"We want to speak to the mayor," she says. "I want to see the mayor here within the hour. He needs to hear our demands."

"The mayor is being evacuated from the city," says the cop. "You'll have to speak to me. You've got four minutes before we go in."

"I told you we will detonate the bomb if you try to come in!" Miss Doomsday says.

"What the fuck is wrong with these people?" Sailboat says to her.

Doomsday shakes her head, then continues.

"All we ask for is to let the people of Crab Town work," she tells the cop. "All we want are jobs. We don't want money, we don't want support. We just want the opportunity to work and get back on our feet."

"You're going to jail for the rest of your lives," the cop says. "They've got plenty of jobs in there for you."

"We're not talking about ourselves. We're doing this for all Crab Town citizens. We want them to have the opportunity to work."

"The citizens of Crab Town do have the opportunity to work just as much as anyone else. If they can't get jobs it's because they don't have the skills and experience needed."

"That's not true," says Miss Doomsday. "Plenty of people here have the skills needed to get jobs. You've made it illegal for companies to hire Crab Town residents."

"There's no law that states companies are not allowed to hire Crab Town citizens."

"It's an unwritten law! You know it's true. Talk to any resident of Crab Town. You'll learn that not a single person here is able to get a job, no matter how educated. Those that did have jobs were fired for no good reason."

"It's not the city's fault. We can't force companies to hire you people."

"We don't want you to force them to hire us. We just want a fair chance."

"You need to come out of there now. This is your final warning."

Miss Doomsday grips her Tommy Gun. She wishes Jack was there with them. He would have been better at convincing them to listen. She's just not convincing enough. She can't find the right words.

"You listen to me!" says Miss Doomsday. "I want to speak to the mayor. You get him back into town. You get him here. If you don't listen to me I will detonate the bomb and then you, me, this entire city, it will be reduced to a pile of ash. Is that what you want? Is that what you're trying to make me do?"

"One minute," the cops say.

"Fuck you!" says Miss Doomsday.

"What are we going to do now?" says Sailboat. "Set off the bomb? Blow up the whole city, all of our friends, all the people in Crab Town?"

"No, of course not," says Doomsday. "Even if we fail, we can't destroy the city. The rest of the House of Cards might find another solution to help the residents of Crab Town. The Four Aces will figure something out, eventually."

"Those assholes are going to break in here shooting," Sailboat says. "They're going to end up detonating the bomb themselves if they're not careful."

When Miss Doomsday looks out of the window, she sees a squad of officers charging the building. They have a battering ram with them. "They're coming."

"What do we do?" Sailboat asks, pumping his shotgun.

Little Sister says, "We can still escape on the sail-bikes. I'm sure we can."

"We're surrounded," Sailboat says. "There's no way out."

"No," she says, pointing out of the window. "Look out by the edge of the square. If we can get there we can take the tunnel out to the bay. We can lose them, I know we can."

"We'll never make it to the tunnel," says Sailboat. "Do you see how many guns are out there?"

Little Sister grinds her fists. "No, I swear we can get there. You just have to trust me."

Johnny Balloon sees a glowing red dot on the girl's chest as she speaks. At first, he thinks it's a trick of the light, but then he recognizes it as a laser sight.

"Get down!" Johnny yells.

He jumps in front of Little Sister just as the sniper fires the weapon. Johnny acts before he thinks, forgetting for a brief moment that he isn't solid anymore. He pops as the bullet passes through his back and hits Little Sister square in the heart.

Miss Doomsday jumps as the balloon man pops. She has no idea what has just happened until she sees his balloon skin spraying through the air like confetti, his gaseous form dissipating like rising dust in the sunlight. Then Miss Doomsday sees the teenaged girl fall to the ground with a bullet wound on her chest. The girl dies instantly. Her blue dreadlocks lie across the floor like a dead squid on the beach.

When Sailboat sees her body on the ground, his eyes fill with rage.

"You motherfuckers!" he screams.

He rips Doomsday's Tommy Gun out of her arms, and fires at the cops out of the window. He tears down a line of them as they charge the building.

Miss Doomsday takes Sailboat's shotgun and runs down the stairs. She can hear the gate splinter open as they break it down with the battering ram.

When she gets downstairs, she goes into the back room with Nine, aiming at the gate from the doorway, ready to fire at the cops who enter.

"Nine, do you think you can fire a weapon?" Miss Doomsday says, without looking at her.

The Nine of Hearts doesn't respond.

"Nine?"

Doomsday turns around to see a cluster of black sewer crabs where Nine had been lying. The crabs are ripping apart her flesh, crawling inside her torso and pulling out her insides. Half of her face is missing. A small crab snaps at an eyeball dangling from its socket. Her pink rib bones can be seen through the mass of black spidery limbs.

She sees that there are more crabs coming out of the storm drain toward Nine, like a row of ants. Doomsday isn't sure if the crabs started eating Nine while she was still alive, but she sure hopes that wasn't the case. She hopes she bled to death long before the crabs got to her.

When the cops break through the gate, Miss Doomsday opens fire. She blasts through the first cop, pumps her shotgun, and blows off the next one's elbow before he can find cover. They shoot back at her, tearing through her abdomen with machinegun fire, knocking her to the ground.

She kicks the door closed.

As she holds in her wounds, lying back on the concrete floor, she stairs up at the ceiling. She can hear Sailboat stomping around up there, firing the Tommy Gun, yelling at the cops below, calling them evil bastards for killing Little Sister. She was just a fifteen-year-old kid. He doesn't understand how they could intentionally do such a thing.

Doomsday hears feet scuttling across the floor in the main room.

"Get the bomb out of here!" shouts one of the cops. "Quickly."

Miss Doomsday's eyes widen. "What?"

She hears some kind of forklift being wheeled into the front room, heading toward the Crab-Bomb.

"No," Miss Doomsday calls out. "You'll detonate the bomb…"

But with a bullet in her lungs, her voice isn't loud enough to be heard. She tries to get up, tries crawling toward the door to stop them.

"Don't do it…" she says.

She can't get off the ground, she can't move.

"We never wanted to blow it up," she says. "Even if we failed there would still be hope."

With one more effort to get off the ground, she realizes that it's not just her wounds that are keeping her down. There are black sewer crabs clawing her flesh, holding her to the ground.

"All we wanted to do was talk," she says, as the crabs crawl across her body.

Upstairs, Sailboat runs out of bullets and begins throwing furniture out the windows at the cops.

"Be careful," says the cops behind the door. "That thing could explode."

"All we wanted was a chance," Miss Doomsday says to

the crabs as they tear into her flesh.

The sound of bullets piercing through Sailboat's face can be heard all the way downstairs.

"Just a fair chance, like everyone else."

A cop yells out, "Not like that! It's going to explode!"

Just before the bomb goes off, Miss Doomsday cries out one last time, with all of her strength, hoping to be heard. But before she can get out even a single word, a black crab tears out her tongue like a child being violently separated from its womb.

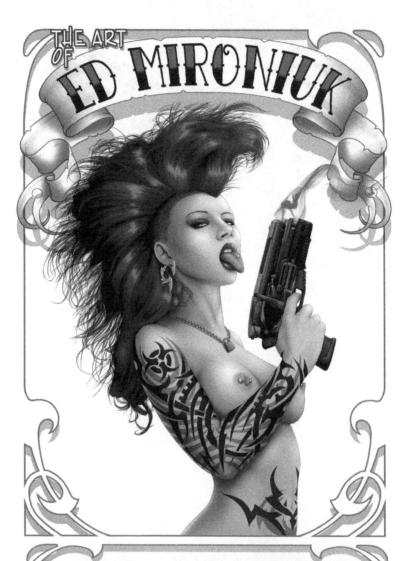

ABOUT THE AUTHOR

Carlton Mellick III is one of the leading authors
in the new *Bizarro* genre uprising. Since 2001,
his surreal counterculture novels have drawn
an international cult following despite the fact
that they have been shunned by most libraries
and corporate bookstores. He lives in Portland,
OR, the bizarro fiction mecca.

Visit him online at **www.carltonmellick.com**

Bizarro books

Bizarro Books publishes under the following imprints:

www.rawdogscreamingpress.com

www.eraserheadpress.co

www.afterbirthbooks.com

www.swallowdownpress.co

For all your Bizarro needs visit:

WWW.BIZARROCENTRAL.COM

Introduce yourselves to the bizarro fiction genre and all of its authors with the Bizarro Starter Kit series. Each volume features short novels and short stories by ten of the leading bizarro authors, designed to give you a perfect sampling of the genre for only $10.

BB-0X1
"The Bizarro Starter Kit" (Orange)
Featuring D. Harlan Wilson, Carlton Mellick III, Jeremy Robert Johnson, Kevin L Donihe, Gina Ranalli, Andre Duza, Vincent W. Sakowski, Steve Beard, John Edward Lawson, and Bruce Taylor.
236 pages $10

BB-0X2
"The Bizarro Starter Kit" (Blue)
Featuring Ray Fracalossy, Jeremy C. Shipp, Jordan Krall, Mykle Hansen, Andersen Prunty, Eckhard Gerdes, Bradley Sands, Steve Aylett, Christian TeBordo, and Tony Rauch. **244 pages $10**

BB-0X2
"The Bizarro Starter Kit" (Purple)
Featuring Russell Edson, Athena Villaverde, David Agranoff, Matthew Revert, Andrew Goldfarb, Jeff Burk, Garrett Cook, Kris Saknussemm, Cody Goodfellow, and Cameron Pierce **264 pages $10**

BB-001 **"The Kafka Effekt" D. Harlan Wilson** - A collection of forty-four irreal short stories loosely written in the vein of Franz Kafka, with more than a pinch of William S. Burroughs sprinkled on top. **211 pages $14**

BB-002 **"Satan Burger" Carlton Mellick III** - The cult novel that put Carlton Mellick III on the map ... Six punks get jobs at a fast food restaurant owned by the devil in a city violently overpopulated by surreal alien cultures. **236 pages $14**

BB-003 **"Some Things Are Better Left Unplugged" Vincent Sakwoski** - Join The Man and his Nemesis, the obese tabby, for a nightmare roller coaster ride into this postmodern fantasy. **152 pages $10**

BB-004 **"Shall We Gather At the Garden?" Kevin L Donihe** - Donihe's Debut novel. Midgets take over the world, The Church of Lionel Richie vs. The Church of the Byrds, plant porn and more! **244 pages $14**

BB-005 **"Razor Wire Pubic Hair" Carlton Mellick III** - A genderless humandildo is purchased by a razor dominatrix and brought into her nightmarish world of bizarre sex and mutilation. **176 pages $11**

BB-006 **"Stranger on the Loose" D. Harlan Wilson** - The fiction of Wilson's 2nd collection is planted in the soil of normalcy, but what grows out of that soil is a dark, witty, otherworldly jungle... **228 pages $14**

BB-007 **"The Baby Jesus Butt Plug" Carlton Mellick III** - Using clones of the Baby Jesus for anal sex will be the hip sex fetish of the future. **92 pages $10**

BB-008 **"Fishyfleshed" Carlton Mellick III** - The world of the past is an illogical flatland lacking in dimension and color, a sick-scape of crispy squid people wandering the desert for no apparent reason. **260 pages $14**

BB-009 "Dead Bitch Army" Andre Duza - Step into a world filled with racist teenagers, cannibals, 100 warped Uncle Sams, automobiles with razor-sharp teeth, living graffiti, and a pissed-off zombie bitch out for revenge. **344 pages $16**

BB-010 "The Menstruating Mall" Carlton Mellick III - "The Breakfast Club meets Chopping Mall as directed by David Lynch." - Brian Keene **212 pages $12**

BB-011 "Angel Dust Apocalypse" Jeremy Robert Johnson - Meth-heads, man-made monsters, and murderous Neo-Nazis. "Seriously amazing short stories..." - Chuck Palahniuk, author of Fight Club **184 pages $11**

BB-012 "Ocean of Lard" Kevin L Donihe / Carlton Mellick III - A parody of those old Choose Your Own Adventure kid's books about some very odd pirates sailing on a sea made of animal fat. **176 pages $12**

BB-015 "Foop!" Chris Genoa - Strange happenings are going on at Dactyl, Inc, the world's first and only time travel tourism company.
"A surreal pie in the face!" - Christopher Moore **300 pages $14**

BB-020 "Punk Land" Carlton Mellick III - In the punk version of Heaven, the anarchist utopia is threatened by corporate fascism and only Goblin, Mortician's sperm, and a blue-mohawked female assassin named Shark Girl can stop them. **284 pages $15**

BB-021"Pseudo-City" D. Harlan Wilson - Pseudo-City exposes what waits in the bathroom stall, under the manhole cover and in the corporate boardroom, all in a way that can only be described as mind-bogglingly irreal. **220 pages $16**

BB-023 "Sex and Death In Television Town" Carlton Mellick III - In the old west, a gang of hermaphrodite gunslingers take refuge from a demon plague in Telos: a town where its citizens have televisions instead of heads. **184 pages $12**

BB-027 **"Siren Promised" Jeremy Robert Johnson & Alan M Clark**
- Nominated for the Bram Stoker Award. A potent mix of bad drugs, bad dreams, brutal bad
guys, and surreal/incredible art by Alan M. Clark. **190 pages $13**

BB-030 **"Grape City" Kevin L. Donihe** - More Donihe-style comedic bizarro
about a demon named Charles who is forced to work a minimum wage job on Earth after
Hell goes out of business. **108 pages $10**

BB-031**"Sea of the Patchwork Cats" Carlton Mellick III** - A quiet
dreamlike tale set in the ashes of the human race. For Mellick enthusiasts who also adore
The Twilight Zone. **112 pages $10**

BB-032 **"Extinction Journals" Jeremy Robert Johnson** - An uncanny
voyage across a newly nuclear America where one man must confront the problems asso-
ciated with loneliness, insane dieties, radiation, love, and an ever-evolving cockroach suit
with a mind of its own. **104 pages $10**

BB-034 **"The Greatest Fucking Moment in Sports" Kevin L. Donihe**
- In the tradition of the surreal anti-sitcom Get A Life comes a tale of triumph and agape
love from the master of comedic bizarro. **108 pages $10**

BB-035 **"The Troublesome Amputee" John Edward Lawson** - Disturb-
ing verse from a man who truly believes nothing is sacred and intends to prove it. **104
pages $9**

BB-037 **"The Haunted Vagina" Carlton Mellick III** - It's difficult to love a
woman whose vagina is a gateway to the world of the dead. **132 pages $10**

BB-042 **"Teeth and Tongue Landscape" Carlton Mellick III** - On a
planet made out of meat, a socially-obsessive monophobic man tries to find his place
amongst the strange creatures and communities that he comes across. **110 pages $10**

BB-043 **"War Slut" Carlton Mellick III** - Part "1984," part "Waiting for Godot," and part action horror video game adaptation of John Carpenter's "The Thing." **116 pages $10**

BB-045 **"Dr. Identity" D. Harlan Wilson** - Follow the Dystopian Duo on a killing spree of epic proportions through the irreal postcapitalist city of Bliptown where time ticks sideways, artificial Bug-Eyed Monsters punish citizens for consumer-capitalist lethargy, and ultraviolence is as essential as a daily multivitamin. **208 pages $15**

BB-047 **"Sausagey Santa" Carlton Mellick III** - A bizarro Christmas tale featuring Santa as a piratey mutant with a body made of sausages. 124 pages $10

BB-048 **"Misadventures in a Thumbnail Universe" Vincent Sakowski** - Dive deep into the surreal and satirical realms of neo-classical Blender Fiction, filled with television shoes and flesh-filled skies. **120 pages $10**

BB-049 **"Vacation" Jeremy C. Shipp** - Blueblood Bernard Johnson leaved his boring life behind to go on The Vacation, a year-long corporate sponsored odyssey. But instead of seeing the world, Bernard is captured by terrorists, becomes a key figure in secret drug wars, and, worse, doesn't once miss his secure American Dream. **160 pages $14**

BB-053 **"Ballad of a Slow Poisoner" Andrew Goldfarb** Millford Mutter-wurst sat down on a Tuesday to take his afternoon tea, and made the unpleasant discovery that his elbows were becoming flatter. **128 pages $10**

BB-055 **"Help! A Bear is Eating Me" Mykle Hansen** - The bizarro, heart-warming, magical tale of poor planning, hubris and severe blood loss... **150 pages $11**

BB-056 **"Piecemeal June" Jordan Krall** - A man falls in love with a living sex doll, but with love comes danger when her creator comes after her with crab-squid assassins. **90 pages $9**

BB-058 **"The Overwhelming Urge" Andersen Prunty** - A collection of bizarro tales by Andersen Prunty. **150 pages $11**

BB-059 **"Adolf in Wonderland" Carlton Mellick III** - A dreamlike adventure that takes a young descendant of Adolf Hitler's design and sends him down the rabbit hole into a world of imperfection and disorder. **180 pages $11**

BB-061 **"Ultra Fuckers" Carlton Mellick III** - Absurdist suburban horror about a couple who enter an upper middle class gated community but can't find their way out. **108 pages $9**

BB-062 **"House of Houses" Kevin L. Donihe** - An odd man wants to marry his house. Unfortunately, all of the houses in the world collapse at the same time in the Great House Holocaust. Now he must travel to House Heaven to find his departed fiancee. **172 pages $11**

BB-064 **"Squid Pulp Blues" Jordan Krall** - In these three bizarro-noir novellas, the reader is thrown into a world of murderers, drugs made from squid parts, deformed gun-toting veterans, and a mischievous apocalyptic donkey. **204 pages $12**

BB-065 **"Jack and Mr. Grin" Andersen Prunty** - "When Mr. Grin calls you can hear a smile in his voice. Not a warm and friendly smile, but the kind that seizes your spine in fear. You don't need to pay your phone bill to hear it. That smile is in every line of Prunty's prose." - Tom Bradley. **208 pages $12**

BB-066 **"Cybernetrix" Carlton Mellick III** - What would you do if your normal everyday world was slowly mutating into the video game world from Tron? **212 pages $12**

BB-072 **"Zerostrata" Andersen Prunty** - Hansel Nothing lives in a tree house, suffers from memory loss, has a very eccentric family, and falls in love with a woman who runs naked through the woods every night. **144 pages $11**

BB-073 **"The Egg Man" Carlton Mellick III** - It is a world where humans reproduce like insects. Children are the property of corporations, and having an enormous ten-foot brain implanted into your skull is a grotesque sexual fetish. Mellick's industrial urban dystopia is one of his darkest and grittiest to date. **184 pages $11**

BB-074 **"Shark Hunting in Paradise Garden" Cameron Pierce** - A group of strange humanoid religious fanatics travel back in time to the Garden of Eden to discover it is invested with hundreds of giant flying maneating sharks. **150 pages $10**

BB-075 **"Apeshit" Carlton Mellick III** - Friday the 13th meets Visitor Q. Six hipster teens go to a cabin in the woods inhabited by a deformed killer. An incredibly fucked-up parody of B-horror movies with a bizarro slant. **192 pages $12**

BB-076 **"Fuckers of Everything on the Crazy Shitting Planet of the Vomit At smosphere" Mykle Hansen** - Three bizarro satires. Monster Cocks, Journey to the Center of Agnes Cuddlebottom, and Crazy Shitting Planet. **228 pages $12**

BB-077 **"The Kissing Bug" Daniel Scott Buck** - In the tradition of Roald Dahl, Tim Burton, and Edward Gorey, comes this bizarro anti-war children's story about a bohemian conenose kissing bug who falls in love with a human woman. **116 pages $10**

BB-078 **"MachoPoni" Lotus Rose** - It's My Little Pony... *Bizarro* style! A long time ago Poniworld was split in two. On one side of the Jagged Line is the Pastel Kingdom, a magical land of music, parties, and positivity. On the other side of the Jagged Line is Dark Kingdom inhabited by an army of undead ponies. **148 pages $11**

BB-079 **"The Faggiest Vampire" Carlton Mellick III** - A Roald Dahl-esque children's story about two faggy vampires who partake in a mustache competition to find out which one is truly the faggiest. **104 pages $10**

BB-080 **"Sky Tongues" Gina Ranalli** - The autobiography of Sky Tongues, the biracial hermaphrodite actress with tongues for fingers. Follow her strange life story as she rises from freak to fame. **204 pages $12**

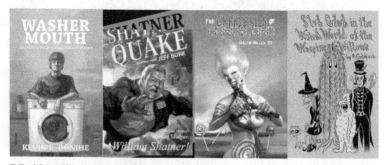

BB-081 **"Washer Mouth" Kevin L. Donihe** - A washing machine becomes human and pursues his dream of meeting his favorite soap opera star. **244 pages $11**

BB-082 **"Shatnerquake" Jeff Burk** - All of the characters ever played by William Shatner are suddenly sucked into our world. Their mission: hunt down and destroy the real William Shatner. **100 pages $10**

BB-083 **"The Cannibals of Candyland" Carlton Mellick III** - There exists a race of cannibals that are made of candy. They live in an underground world made out of candy. One man has dedicated his life to killing them all. **170 pages $11**

BB-084 **"Slub Glub in the Weird World of the Weeping Willows" Andrew Goldfarb** - The charming tale of a blue glob named Slub Glub who helps the weeping willows whose tears are flooding the earth. There are also hyenas, ghosts, and a voodoo priest **100 pages $10**

BB-085 **"Super Fetus" Adam Pepper** - Try to abort this fetus and he'll kick your ass! **104 pages $10**

BB-086 **"Fistful of Feet" Jordan Krall** - A bizarro tribute to spaghetti westerns, featuring Cthulhu-worshipping Indians, a woman with four feet, a crazed gunman who is obsessed with sucking on candy, Syphilis-ridden mutants, sexually transmitted tattoos, and a house devoted to the freakiest fetishes. **228 pages $12**

BB-087 **"Ass Goblins of Auschwitz" Cameron Pierce** - It's Monty Python meets Nazi exploitation in a surreal nightmare as can only be imagined by Bizarro author Cameron Pierce. **104 pages $10**

BB-088 **"Silent Weapons for Quiet Wars" Cody Goodfellow** - "This is high-end psychological surrealist horror meets bottom-feeding low-life crime in a techno-thrilling science fiction world full of Lovecraft and magic..." -John Skipp **212 pages $12**

BB-089 "Warrior Wolf Women of the Wasteland" Carlton Mellick III
Road Warrior Werewolves versus McDonaldland Mutants...post-apocalyptic fiction has never been quite like this. **316 pages $13**

BB-090 "Cursed" Jeremy C Shipp - The story of a group of characters who believe they are cursed and attempt to figure out who cursed them and why. A tale of stylish absurdism and suspenseful horror. **218 pages $15**

BB-091 "Super Giant Monster Time" Jeff Burk - A tribute to choose your own adventures and Godzilla movies. Will you escape the giant monsters that are rampaging the fuck out of your city and shit? Or will you join the mob of alien-controlled punk rockers causing chaos in the streets? What happens next depends on you. **188 pages $12**

BB-092 "Perfect Union" Cody Goodfellow - "Cronenberg's THE FLY on a grand scale: human/insect gene-spliced body horror, where the human hive politics are as shocking as the gore." -John Skipp. **272 pages $13**

BB-093 "Sunset with a Beard" Carlton Mellick III - 14 stories of surreal science fiction. **200 pages $12**

BB-094 "My Fake War" Andersen Prunty - The absurd tale of an unlikely soldier forced to fight a war that, quite possibly, does not exist. It's Rambo meets Waiting for Godot in this subversive satire of American values and the scope of the human imagination. **128 pages $11**

BB-095 "Lost in Cat Brain Land" Cameron Pierce - Sad stories from a surreal world. A fascist mustache, the ghost of Franz Kafka, a desert inside a dead cat. Primordial entities mourn the death of their child. The desperate serve tea to mysterious creatures. A hopeless romantic falls in love with a pterodactyl. And much more. **152 pages $11**

BB-096 "The Kobold Wizard's Dildo of Enlightenment +2" Carlton Mellick III - A Dungeons and Dragons parody about a group of people who learn they are only made up characters in an AD&D campaign and must find a way to resist their nerdy teenaged players and retarded dungeon master in order to survive. 232 **pages $12**

BB-097 **"My Heart Said No, but the Camera Crew Said Yes!" Bradley Sands** - A collection of short stories that are crammed with the delightfully odd and the scurrilously silly. **140 pages $13**

BB-098 **"A Hundred Horrible Sorrows of Ogner Stump" Andrew Goldfarb** - Goldfarb's acclaimed comic series. A magical and weird journey into the horrors of everyday life. **164 pages $11**

BB-099 **"Pickled Apocalypse of Pancake Island" Cameron Pierce** A demented fairy tale about a pickle, a pancake, and the apocalypse. **102 pages $8**

BB-100 **"Slag Attack" Andersen Prunty** - Slag Attack features four visceral, noir stories about the living, crawling apocalypse.A slag is what survivors are calling the slug-like maggots raining from the sky, burrowing inside people, and hollowing out their flesh and their sanity. **148 pages $11**

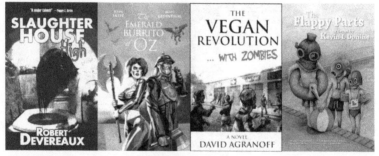

BB-101 **"Slaughterhouse High" Robert Devereaux** - A place where schools are built with secret passageways, rebellious teens get zippers installed in their mouths and genitals, and once a year, on that special night, one couple is slaughtered and the bits of their bodies are kept as souvenirs. **304 pages $13**

BB-102 **"The Emerald Burrito of Oz" John Skipp & Marc Levinthal** OZ IS REAL! Magic is real! The gate is really in Kansas! And America is finally allowing Earth tourists to visit this weird-ass, mysterious land. But when Gene of Los Angeles heads off for summer vacation in the Emerald City, little does he know that a war is brewing...a war that could destroy both worlds. **280 pages $13**

BB-103 **"The Vegan Revolution... with Zombies"** David Agranoff When there's no more meat in hell, the vegans will walk the earth. **160 pages $11**

BB-104 **"The Flappy Parts" Kevin L Donihe** - Poems about bunnies, LSD, and police abuse. You know, things that matter. **132 pages $11**

BB-105 "Sorry I Ruined Your Orgy" Bradley Sands - Bizarro humorist
**Bradley Sands returns with one of the strangest, most hilarious collections of the year.
130 pages $11**

BB-106 "Mr. Magic Realism" Bruce Taylor - Like Golden Age science fiction comics written by Freud, *Mr. Magic Realism* is a strange, insightful adventure that spans the furthest reaches of the galaxy, exploring the hidden caverns in the hearts and minds of men, women, aliens, and biomechanical cats. **152 pages $11**

BB-107 "Zombies and Shit" Carlton Mellick III - "Battle Royale" meets "Return of the Living Dead." Mellick's bizarro tribute to the zombie genre. **308 pages $13**

BB-108 "The Cannibal's Guide to Ethical Living" Mykle Hansen - Over a five star French meal of fine wine, organic vegetables and human flesh, a lunatic delivers a witty, chilling, disturbingly sane argument in favor of eating the rich.. **184 pages $11**

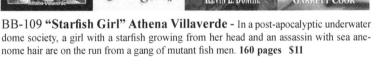

BB-109 "Starfish Girl" Athena Villaverde - In a post-apocalyptic underwater dome society, a girl with a starfish growing from her head and an assassin with sea anenome hair are on the run from a gang of mutant fish men. **160 pages $11**

BB-110 "Lick Your Neighbor" Chris Genoa - Mutant ninjas, a talking whale, kung fu masters, maniacal pilgrims, and an alcoholic clown populate Chris Genoa's surreal, darkly comical and unnerving reimagining of the first Thanksgiving. **303 pages $13**

BB-111 "Night of the Assholes" Kevin L. Donihe - A plague of assholes is infecting the countryside. Normal everyday people are transforming into jerks, snobs, dicks, and douchebags. And they all have only one purpose: to make your life a living hell.. **192 pages $11**

BB-112 "Jimmy Plush, Teddy Bear Detective" Garrett Cook - Hardboiled cases of a private detective trapped within a teddy bear body. **180 pages $11**

CPSIA information can be obtained
at www.ICGtesting.com
Printed in the USA
LVHW101305220522
719207LV00007BA/344